For Rosemary

Marguerite Bell (Ida Pollock) began writing when she was 10 years old. Breaking into print a few years later she seemed destined for early success, but illness and the outbreak of World War II placed a check on her career. In 1943 she married Hugh Pollock, a charismatic soldier and publisher who had previously been married to Enid Blyton, and life settled down for a while. However, after the war she started writing again, quickly acquiring five publishers and a million readers worldwide. With over one hundred novels to her name, written under various pseudonyms, she has enjoyed numerous successes.

She has travelled widely, living in several different countries, but has now settled in a quiet village in south Cornwall. In addition to writing, she is also a talented artist, and has had her work in oils accepted accepted for national exhibition.

Ida is still writing in 2008, at the remarkable age of 100 years. She has one daughter, Rosemary, who is also a writer.

I

The notepaper was rose pink and scented, the cramped handwriting had been blotched by tears. With some reluctance, Fanny Templeton passed her stepdaughter's letter to the woman seated beside her.

"You may see what she has written, ma'am."

"H'mm. . . . What age is your stepdaughter, did you say?"

"She is nineteen. ma'am."

"Not very old, to be sure, but she's married now and enceinte, and must put up with the situation. Now pray put the silly girl out of your head, it will soon be time for Pug to take his walk."

"Ma'am, I cannot put Justine out of my head."

"Why not? This young woman married against your wishes and will have to live with the consequences. In this world, my dear, we must all endeavour to support our own difficulties. As you are doing. You are a widow – at the age of six and twenty - and have been cast upon the world with nothing. I pay you a wage and so you survive. But do you whimper? Do you complain, and write begging letters to your relations?"

"Justine's situation is different, ma'am. She is living in a strange place, without friends. And she is not much more than a child herself."

"Nonsense! When I last saw her - two years ago, was it not? - she looked older than you do now. A hulking, long-limbed lump of a girl. That husband of hers must have been having problems with his eyesight. Now really, I have heard enough of this!"

She tossed the letter aside, and it fluttered to the floor. As Fanny gathered it up the scent caused her nose to wrinkle, and she wondered why her employer had not commented on such a manifestation of vulgarity, but that was typical of Lady Mapleforth. Sharp-tongued and out-spoken as she could often be, she was also capable of astonishing tact. She was kind-hearted, too – though it had never been likely that she would feel much sympathy for Justine.

Poor Justine. It was not easy to imagine Giles's carefree, cosseted daughter living in some hovel of an apartment in Bath. With a half-pay captain for a husband and tormented by all the unpleasantness of a difficult pregnancy – morning sickness, palpitations, weakness and a shocking loss of figure – it was hardly surprising she was so distressed.

As if thinking aloud, Fanny said: "If only poor Freddie had not been wounded. It's an injury that refuses to heal."

Lady Mapelforth sighed. "Practically every decent young officer has been wounded during the last few years, and no doubt quite a lot are not healing up very well. In time, I daresay, the young man will make a complete recovery, but until that happens his wife must learn to manage. They did not have to marry in such tremendous haste - why was there so much hurry, I should like to know? Why did they not at least wait until the poor boy's leg was nearly well?" A lorgnette was lifted to piercingly bright grey eyes. "Did they not elope together. . . ? Quite probably the stupid girl was already in an interesting condition."

"No, no." In spite of those two years of marriage, Fanny felt herself blushing. "The whole thing was arranged without proper discussion, but that was mainly because Freddie had been ordered back to his regiment. Did. . . did you know, ma'am, that

Freddie is a younger brother of Lord Ordley?"

"Yes, I have heard that, and I must say I feel very sorry for men who find themselves burdened by troublesome younger brothers."

It was now or never. Fanny had made up her mind to be strong for Justine – she owed that much to her late husband – and this was her opportunity. Freddie, apparently, had made several appeals to his brother already, but so far these had fallen upon deaf ears. She herself had written to the Marquis, but had received no reply. If she were to confront him, though – and she was, after all, his sister-in-law's stepmamma – he would surely have to do something.

"I am sure," she said firmly, "Lord Ordley would wish to help Freddie, if only he understood all the circumstances. I think, ma'am, you said he is coming to dine here this evening."

"Yes, that is quite correct - " Lady Mapelforth broke off, and the lorgnette slipped. "No! Fanny, I forbid it! The Marquis of Ordley will not be troubled while he is under my roof. It is unthinkable! Unthinkable, do you understand?" There was a pause, broken only by the rhythmic snoring of Pug, and she went on more gently: "I understand that you feel a sense of family obligation. Perhaps I should not say so, but I disapprove very strongly of men who leave their wives and daughters unprovided for. After barely two years of wedlock you were made a widow, then almost before you had been fitted for your weeds you were obliged to go out and seek your own living. To tell the truth it is a thankful thing that girl insisted upon marrying against your advice, for otherwise you would be supporting her as well as yourself. Now you really must abandon her to the husband she was so determined to acquire, and put your own concerns to the foremost."

"But you see," Fanny said quietly, "I have an affection for Justine, and I am afraid her health is in danger. Also the health of her infant."

"Why?" Lady Mapelforth demanded.

"Well, they really have very little to eat. I am quite certain about that. I understand that you would not wish Lord Ordley to be approached while he is dining here, and naturally I shan't speak to him – on that occasion – if you don't wish it. I shall simply go to his house."

"You will not do anything of the kind. Every woman needs to be careful of her reputation, and young widows should be warier than most. If you go to Ordley's house people will imagine they know very well what to think, and that kind of thing, believe me, is not to be lived down."

Fanny was silent, and Lady Mapelforth spread her plump fingers in a gesture of despair.

"Oh, very well! Since you are so obstinate, you may speak to Ordley when he comes here. I suppose you had better take him into the library. Just in case you should be observed by anyone, I will make it known there is family business between you. Just don't remain alone with him for too long, and for heaven's sake don't make him angry."

As Pug's snoring reached a crescendo, Fanny's eyes lit up.

"Thank you, Lady Mapelforth! Now, shall I take Pug for his walk in the Park?"

II

When Fanny returned from the Park she would have liked very much to spend a little time thinking about the evening ahead, but there was too much to be done and as soon as she had finished re-stringing her employer's pearls – not for the first time – she made her way down to the kitchens.

Since the death of her own husband three years earlier Lady Mapelforth had been unable to entertain as she had once been accustomed to do, but every so often her bachelor brother arrived to stay, and when this happened he came in very handy as a temporary host. Her dinner parties, planned to coincide with Sir Timothy's not infrequent visits, were as successful as they had always been and the host's taciturnity was if anything an advantage, or so Lady Mapelforth thought. In her present situation Fanny usually found such occasions a little difficult, not that this was the fault of her employer. In public, at least, the temperamental dowager contrived for most of the time to treat her companion like a daughter.

Going down into the kitchens, Fanny offered her assistance to Cook. The lower regions of the house had been invaded by sinister emanations from the big roasting oven, and it appeared two ducks had recently been reduced to cinders, while a side of lamb was in danger of going the same way. Cook – who had not long recovered from a nasty fall on the stairs and in any case detested formal dinner parties - was inclined, through her tears, to blame the stupid girl whose duty it had been to attend the oven. The stupid girl, herself also in tears, was attempting to resuscitate the ducks. Fanny, who had been called upon to perform such functions before, whipped the lamb out of the oven, rescued a tray of strawberry tartlets and a gooseberry pie from another oven, then went on to recover the cook with a small glass of porter and the kitchen-maid with a mild lecture. Having ordered all the windows to be opened, she then separated Pug from a chicken carcass which he had discovered in the outer scullery. Restored more or less to herself, Cook resumed control of the preparations and Fanny was at last able to escape.

Flying upstairs to her room, she hastily examined the contents of her wardrobe, deciding eventually upon a simple lavender-coloured muslin. Its waist bound by narrow black velvet ribbon, it was the first thing she had acquired after emerging from the long months of mourning for Giles. She knew that it suited her, but at the same time it was discreet. She wanted to look well that evening, but not as if she were attempting to be something she could not be.

So far she had met Lord Ordley just once. Rather unexpectedly he had attended his brother's quiet, hurried wedding, and on that occasion it had not been easy to speak with him. When confronted by strangers – persons such as herself, at any rate – he tended to stare, brows crinkling slightly, as if puzzled such a curious object should have been thrust upon his attention, and once a few sentences had been exchanged boredom quickly began to show. He was, she recalled, undeniably handsome, but at the same time his face was dark and forbidding. She would have been more than happy to avoid crossing his path again.

This further meeting, though, could not be avoided, and as she studied her reflection in a looking-glass she began to feel reasonably satisfied with the way she looked. For a young, hard-up widow who had no particular wish to attract attention she was suitably and pleasingly dressed.

Glancing out of her window she saw the first carriage rattle to a halt far below, then as its occupants were admitted by Caldicott the butler some other gentleman stepped from an old-fashioned sedan. It was probably time to go downstairs.

Before changing her gown Fanny had slipped down to inspect the dining-room, and she knew it could hardly have looked more splendid. Silver and crystal glittered, and bowls of late roses filled the room with their scent. Everything was in order, and when Lady Mapelforth finally descended in her black satin and lace it would be hard for her to find any kind of fault.

Fanny opened her door and stepped out on to the landing, and at that moment a masculine voice drifted up from the lobby two floors below. It was a voice she knew, and to her annoyance the fingers that grasped her fan began to tremble. Lord Ordley, it seemed, was among the very first arrivals.

Downstairs she hesitated outside the drawing-room door. Inside, guests were sipping sherry and ratafia and chattering like the inhabitants of a well conducted but over-crowded aviary – the ladies' voices, shrill and insistent, soaring above the hearty baritone laughter of their male companions. Judging by their extreme affability, it seemed likely some of the gentlemen had recently emerged from neighbouring Clubs, and partly for this reason Fanny decided she would not join the gathering until after it had filed into the dining-room.

When at last they had taken their places she slipped into her allotted position near the bottom of the table and found her immediate neighbour was an innocuous young cleric with little to say for himself. This could have been tedious, but it did at least leave her with plenty of opportunity to observe the other guests, most of whom she had met on at least one previous occasion. Lady Palfrey, a vivacious widow, had two very pretty daughters, both of whom had recently come out. Then there was a young captain of Dragoons, a retired admiral who wished only to discuss the last century's naval engagements, and a Member of Parliament – Robert Dawkins - whose dowdy young wife seemed as anxious as Fanny to escape attention.

And there was Colonel the Marquis of Ordley, seated next to his hostess at the top end of the table. If Lady Mapelforth had expected him to honour the occasion by making his appearance in full regimentals she could have been forgiven for feeling a touch of disappointment, for he was quite soberly dressed in a coat of grey velvet, but the coat was beautifully cut. The lace at his neck and wrists could only have come from Mechlin, and a large ruby embedded in the folds of his cravat sent out shafts of fire that drew attention to his unusually firm chin, while another ruby flashed on the little finger of his right hand. His dark hair had been brushed into a perfect Brutus, and if anything he looked more handsome than Fanny remembered. It was hardly surprising that Lady Mapelforth, though middle-aged and of mountainous proportions, found herself flushing like a girl every time she encountered her guest's lustrous dark eyes. And when he leaned towards her, murmuring some small witticism, she could not prevent herself tittering as noisily as any of those mindless females she normally deplored.

Fanny could hardly believe her ears when the shrill volume of laughter reached her, and she tried to reconcile the Lord Ordley she was seeing tonight with the man she had encountered at Justine's wedding. Tonight he was all urbanity, relaxed and whimsical and teasing, and the two Palfrey girls were plainly entranced. The captain of Dragoons, beside whom one of them had been seated, could hardly hope to hold their interest at all when this devastating exquisite – a Marquis *and* a soldier – had been placed just a few feet away. On top of everything else Ordley was a man of maturity and experience, and during the recent wars he had seen a great deal of conflict, not that he seemed in the least eager to talk about that. He was in a mood to be flirtatious, and as his gaze dwelt upon the Misses Palfrey they could have been forgiven for assuming he found their simple charms decidedly seductive.

Lady Mapelforth's dinner parties had never been known to be anything but successful, and this one had a particularly good mixture of ingredients. Only at the bottom of the table – where the host, her ladyship's brother, was evidently on the edge of sleep - did silence brood persistently, and after a time it did begin to strike Fanny as a little odd she and the inarticulate clergyman could be so persistently disregarded. Eyeing the young man next to her she wondered, at one stage, whether she should strive to remember a quotation or two from St Paul, perhaps concerning the female sex since he did seem to be something of a misogynist - on the other hand, she could be wrong about that. Having seen him glance surreptitiously at the Bishop's young and very pretty wife it struck her he might just possibly be suffering from a secret and hopeless infatuation; until the arrival of the salmon trout - accompanied by sweetbreads and mushrooms - brought such a beam of hope to his face she immediately dismissed this theory, accepting instead he was simply undernourished.

And at the very same moment she intercepted a look from the Marquis of Ordley. It had travelled the length of the table, by-passing twin mountains of fruit and flowers and remaining fixed upon her for several seconds. There was no recognition, though, in the look. It was simply a cool, hard stare, accompanied by that faint crinkling of the eyebrows.

The Naval gentleman began to talk about Europe, inviting his neighbours to comment on portentous discussions that were rumoured to be going on in Vienna. The map of Europe was being re-drawn, and the wide world was going to be affected. Names such as Metternich, Castlereagh and Talleyrand began to be bandied about, and even the hungry clergyman started to take an interest, eagerly declaring his personal distrust of Metternich. The Captain of Dragoons remarked that the situation seemed fraught with grave problems, perhaps even danger. . . Napoleon Buonaparte might now be locked up on the island of Elba, but that did not mean there would never again be war in Europe. Indeed, if the Allied nations were to persist with their present disagreements war might be forced upon them all before long.

At the mention of Napoleon's name Lady Palfrey and both her daughters let out protesting shrieks, and Lady Mapelforth wagged an admonitory finger at the officer.

"You are a man of war, Captain Maitland, and I am afraid you dream of war. Now they have that dreadful Buonaparte held fast upon Elba why should we feel the need to be apprehensive in any way? I, for one, shall not lie shivering in my bed at night because some other upstart may one day see fit to invade us."

"Hear, hear," Robert Hawkins applauded gruffly, at the same time accepting a strawberry tartlet.

Deciding it was time she said something that could be regarded as arresting, the older Miss Palfrey remarked she would like to travel abroad.

"Above everything I'd wish to see Rome, and Venice, and Florence, and - and Geneva. And Paris. I am certain one would be quite secure, for they say the countryside is not nearly so bad as one might imagine. The people, poor things, are thin and starved and of course the inns are unbelievably dirty. But Paris is splendid, with wonderful buildings and parks and squares – and whole avenues of orange trees, think of that! People sit about under the trees, sipping their drinks and watching tumblers and puppet shows, just as if there had never been a war! There are triumphal arches everywhere, and the theatres are packed. And then the ladies are so fashionable! I would give anything to own a gown made in Paris."

"Mamma," her sister remarked, "has said that we may go to France as soon as Christmas is over. Is that not so, mamma?"

Lady Palfrey smiled dotingly at both girls. "It is indeed, my love. Only perhaps not immediately after Christmas. I think we should wait until the weather is a little warmer."

"I would choose to visit the *south* of France," Lady Mapelforth put in. "I believe it is quite a paradise, and very warm. I have a friend, a charming Frenchwoman who fled the country after that dreadful rebellion. She has recovered her house near Marseilles but does not wish to visit there any more. I have been invited to go and stay, if I wish. It is in good order, and there are servants in the house. I own, on these wintry days I am very much tempted." She turned to the Marquis. "What do you say, my lord?"

Ordley shrugged his elegant shoulders.

"It is not for me to advise you, Lady Mapelforth, but I would suggest you remember France has been in turmoil for more than twenty years. The Revolution all but destroyed ordinary life, and then the wars began. Buonaparte did much for the country, re-built its laws, its style of government - even the city of Paris," with a half smile at the senior Miss Palfrey. "If he had been content to remain within his own borders all might have been well, but of course he felt the need to over-run and dominate all his neighbours, and so we had to oppose him. It's true the villain is now locked away safely, but no more than a few months ago we were still fighting within French territory, and that leaves scars on a country. Unless you have urgent reasons, I would think twice about venturing there too soon." He set about preparing a peach for his hostess. "Of course, the scenery is next to none, but the roads are. . . hazardous. To say the least. Who would accompany you, ma'am?"

"Why, Mrs Templeton. . . I should not stir without her. And my maid, and I think Caldicott, since one must have someone who can control a household. But I really don't see, sir," accepting the peach, "how there can possibly be very much danger. Why, many French people are now going back to recover their homes and their estates."

"Which in many cases no longer exist. Numberless fine houses have been razed to the ground by fire and the viciousness of the peasantry. I give you my word, Lady Mapelforth, the land-owning classes in France have suffered in a way you might find it difficult to imagine. Some people feel they have been justly punished for past abuses of power, but if you had seen what I have seen. . . ."

Becoming aware of the fact several ladies were staring at him with widened eyes, he shrugged again and smiled. "In a few months' time, no doubt, the whole continent of Europe will be safe once more. Journeys of pleasure should, perhaps, be postponed until then."

"There!" exclaimed the older Miss Palfrey. "I am entirely in the right of it. *Very* soon now we shall be able to travel just as we like, and there will be no more of your horrid wars." Gazing straight at the Marquis, she fluttered her eyelashes. "I believe you soldiers think of nothing else, I truly do."

In the drawing-room Fanny took up a position behind the tea-tray. Attempting – as she said later – to find out what could be wrong with the poor creature, Lady Mapelforth sat down beside Mrs Hawkins, and as Lady Palfrey settled in a corner with the Bishop's wife her older daughter arranged herself in what was presumably meant to be a classic pose. Meanwhile her sister attacked the piano, her aggressively executed arpeggios rolling on relentlessly until the gentlemen started to appear, when she wavered and came to a halt.

As they left the dining-room Lady Mapelforth had intimated, in an undertone, that she had 'everything arranged', but it was impossible for Fanny to know exactly what this meant and by the time Lord Ordley appeared in the drawing-room her nerves were getting close to breaking point. Her hands shook as she manipulated the sugar tongs, and at one point the enormous silver tea-pot was in danger of disgorging its entire contents on to the tea tray.

She heard the Marquis decline a cup of tea, and then she heard his hostess declare loudly she had not forgotten their earlier conversation. Mrs Templeton would conduct him to the library, where he would almost certainly discover the volume they had been discussing. It might very likely be on one of the higher shelves, but the steps, of course, would be there, and Mrs Templeton would help him to find it. She was forever browsing in the library. "Is that not so, Fanny, my dear?"

Fanny was so startled she was quite sure she betrayed the fact. Lady Mapelforth was rattling on about an extract, bound in vellum, from somebody's history of the Trojan wars – it was a rare volume, she believed, and something much prized by her husband. The author was excessively well known, only his name had escaped her again.

"Herodotus," his lordship suggested helpfully.

"Yes, of course, to be sure. You are very right, sir. I have already asked Caldicott to ensure there is a sufficiency of candles lit in the library, and if more are needed Fanny must send for them." She turned and beckoned imperiously. "Fanny! Take Lord Ordley to the library, if you please, and help him to find this book we have been talking about."

For several seconds Fanny stared at her blankly, then she recognised that she had a double duty ahead of her, and there was no way out of it. She herself had contrived at this situation, and now had to face what lay ahead. She turned and led the way out of the drawing-room, and his lordship followed with purposeful footsteps. Firmly, he closed the door behind them.

In the library there certainly was a considerable blaze of candles, and feeling inclined to tackle the simpler task first Fanny made for one of the lower bookshelves beside the fireplace. But Lord Ordley's voice stopped her.

"Never mind the book, young woman. The Persian wars have never interested me in the slightest, but I do want to know whether you and I have met before. I am convinced that we have. When was it, and where?"

Fanny turned and stared at him. "You mean to say you do not recollect?"

He shook his head. "No."

"Yet for some reason you feel that you ought to know me?"

"I have an uneasy feeling that *you* consider I ought to know you." His voice was as impatient as the look on his face, and both suggested he had been nurturing a considerable degree of resentment, all for some obscure reason connected with the fact that she had been present in the same company as himself. Which seemed somewhat illogical, if he hadn't the faintest idea who she was.

"You had better tell me where it was that we last met." His tone was crisp. "Were you serving a useful purpose in some other household? I suppose you may have been a governess, but it's more probable that you were serving as a companion. I have little to do with governesses. At any rate, if I once offended you in some way you had better tell me how it came about."

"You did not offend me, sir." She was so indignant that her voice quivered. "And I can assure you that I have never acted as companion to anyone save Lady Mapelforth. I *was* once a governess, but that was some time ago. . . when I was engaged by my late husband to take charge of your sister-in-law."

His eyebrows shot up. "My sister-in-law?"

"Your brother Freddie's wife, Justine. I was once her governess, but three years ago I became her stepmamma. You last saw me, sir, when we were both in attendance at your brother's wedding. There were so few other guests, and the circumstances were so. . .unusual that I cannot believe you have forgotten the occasion entirely. Though I admit there is no reason why you should particularly remember me."

"On the contrary," he drawled, "I think most men would remember you, with that striking red hair and those angry green eyes. But since it's clear that I cannot have had the honour of being introduced, can we now put the matter right, Mrs. . . er. . .?"

"I am Frances Templeton, the widow of Giles Templeton, Justine's father." Her back was ramrod stiff. "Sadly my husband died two years ago. If he had lived, I am very sure such an unfortunate marriage would never have taken place."

"Indeed? You mean he would have consigned the girl to a nunnery?"

"I mean that my husband had very little money, and he did not wish Justine to mix with fashionable young men. But when – when he died I permitted her to stay with friends who were launching their own daughter upon society, and it was there that she met your brother - "

"Ah! So that was how it happened." He was surveying her coolly, with a kind of detached interest. "I have sometimes wondered, since she was not 'out', as the expression goes. And having met they made a decision to elope?"

"That was most unfortunate. I could not feel more strongly about it."

"Nor I." He had started wandering about the room, taking books from the shelves and putting them back again, snuffing out a guttering candle. "I was, and am outraged. Freddie was compromised almost from the moment he set eyes on that girl. Your stepdaughter, Mrs Templeton, is the kind of idiotic young woman whose head contains nothing but the kind of stuff that can be imbibed from novels. Gretna Green and a hired chaise. . . angry father in pursuit. Only in this case there was no angry father. Only you, Mrs Templeton, the wretched chit's useless stepmother."

Fanny stared at him. She was so astonished that the insult almost slipped over her head. How could he possibly think she was to blame?

"If I had known of the affair," she said slowly, "I would have done everything in my power to stop what was happening. But Justine was staying with my husband's oldest friends, and they knew nothing. Freddie was there because the son, Mr Edmund Andrews, was – is - one of his brother officers, and both young men were on leave. I believe it was Edmund who arranged matters for Freddie, obtaining the hired chaise, and so on. He refused to tell his father where they had gone, and I knew nothing until twelve hours later I received a message from Mr Andrews. About the same time. . . ." Her voice wavered. It was hard to go on without reliving some of the torment she had endured that day. "About the same time a post came from Justine, telling me they had arrived in Collington. She said that Freddie wanted to press ahead for Gretna Green, but that she – she did not want to be married without my blessing." Without looking at him, Fanny went on: "They had spent the night together, at the inn in Collington. It was very much too late. But all of this you must remember."

"Indeed." He went on dryly: "I never had any doubt that Freddie waited until your stepdaughter was abed then crept in with averted eyes to take his rest in the fireplace, but the world is not likely to believe that, and so a young man's life has been destroyed."

"That is hardly true, Lord Ordley." Her mouth felt dry, and she wondered how much longer she would be able to go on with this. She had to go on with it, though. She still had a request to make.

He had returned to the middle of the room and was standing within a few paces of her, his superior height making her five feet, seven and a half inches seem utterly insignificant. Looking up, she saw sparks of fury in his eyes.

"Mrs Templeton, my brother is a promising officer. He has no inherited money because my father believed a younger son should strive to build his own fortune, but he has the ability to win swift promotion and just now should be giving his mind to nothing else. He should not have been married for at least another five years - at his age, he should not be wasting his time on family problems or financial difficulties. This absurd union with your stepdaughter will have done incalculable damage to his prospects."

"One could say that at his age he should not have to cope with a shattered leg which refuses to mend." Fanny's voice was cold. "With or without an impoverished wife, just now he is hardly in any position to concentrate on winning promotion. Freddie, it seems to me, is in need of support. . . from his family."

The Marquis stood still, frowning at her.

"Have you," he demanded, "any idea what you are saying? It is I who have been attempting to pick up the pieces. Your stepdaughter appears quite incapable of managing household finances, and I have been obliged to offer them considerable assistance. Lady Freddie spends money like water, and bills from her dressmaker reach me by practically every post, to say nothing of grocers', butchers' and vintners' bills. My brother clearly feels a sense of shame, but of course he never offers the smallest criticism of his wife. A few months ago I installed them in a cottage on one of my estates, and so that their child, when it arrives, shall not be inconvenienced by rats or damp I have had it gutted and re-furbished for them." He paused, and drew breath. "You know, Mrs Templeton, I have a feeling that you planned to waylay me this evening. To offer an appeal on behalf of your relative and her unfortunate husband. If obliged to confront your anxiety and distress – you probably thought - my stony indifference might soften." He glanced briefly at her startled face. "All her appeals have been ignored, have they not? To say nothing of requests from my brother. Obliged to contemplate giving birth in some revolting hovel – complete with threadbare carpets and duns at the door – Freddie's hapless young wife has been driven to the edge of insanity, or something like that. Has a familiar ring, does it not?"

Fanny was so dumbfounded that for nearly half a minute she was unable to speak. "I can't believe it," she said at last. "Only the other day I had a letter – "

"I'm quite sure you did. That girl is entirely without conscience. Marriage to Freddie may improve her, but I doubt it. Personally I find it impossible to discover anything, either in or about her, which could account for my brother's continuing infatuation. His one desire is to please her on every occasion. . . she has him in thrall, and it is something I despise in him. No man should be as weak as that. Certainly not in my family."

Fanny gazed at him. She could hardly believe that Justine had misled her in such a way. Lord Ordley could scarcely be lying, certainly not about the re-furbished cottage on one of his own estates. But all those letters. . . . According to Justine she had been forced to accept the loan of a crib, not to mention several other vital necessities, and could see no hope at all of being able to buy lace for a christening robe. And then, she was living in such depressing surroundings. According to the local physician, she was not sufficiently well nourished to expect anything but a difficult confinement.

Then Fanny recollected the scented, expensive notepaper. At last, she asked: "But where are they living? I have been writing to an address in Bath."

Walking over to a small desk, Lord Ordley took up a sheet of notepaper. He wrote something on it, then carried the scrap of paper over to Fanny.

"Rose Lodge," he said crisply. "It is situated close to Whitcombe Park, in the county of Somerset. No doubt one of my men has been going at regular intervals to collect their correspondence from Bath, but your letters should now be addressed to Whitcombe. The lodge was in a fairly dilapidated state, but I can assure you it has now been converted into a suitable bower for your stepdaughter and her family – though Lady Freddie, of course, may still feel it is not quite what she expected when she married into my family. No doubt she has it in mind already that her child, if a boy, may one day inherit the Ordley estates. I and my first brother, Hugh, are both in the Service and since neither of us has yet succumbed to matrimony. . .who knows?"

Fanny didn't answer. She was staring at the paper in her hand, and the bold script that said so much about his lordship. Firm, clear and purposeful, without so much as an ornamental twirl to detract from its incisive message. She could imagine that same signature being appended, without a moment's hesitation, to legal documents and important communiquès – he would never hesitate, so long as his mind and conscience believed he was doing the right thing.

"I suggest," he was saying, "that you ask Lady Mapelforth if she might be willing to dispense with your services for a few days, so that you can hire a chaise and travel into Somerset. Only in that way, I imagine, will you be able to reassure yourself that Lady Freddie's present privations are not quite what you feared."

Shocked as she was by Justine's distortion of the truth, Fanny could not help feeling resentment. Lord Ordley's contempt, both for her and for her late husband's family, was obvious and difficult to endure. The fact was, though, that he had been seriously and unjustly maligned.

"I must thank you," she said awkwardly, "for everything you have done. I admit that I had no idea - and it is true that I had planned, this evening, to ask for your help. As you suggest, I shall travel toWhitcombe. And if things are as you say, I shall make my stepdaughter understand that she is fortunate."

He bowed.

"Unaccustomed as I am to having my word so openly doubted, I do understand that your position is far from easy. Having acquired a husband who was either unable or unwilling to make adequate provision for your security after his death, it seems that you are now burdened by a spoilt, hysterical and unreliable daughter. Which leads me to make a recommendation that you are undoubtedly going to resent."

He had paused directly in front of her, and she found herself staring fixedly at the ruby in his cravat. Afraid that he was going to say something outrageous, she felt herself stiffen; then suddenly he lifted a hand to touch one of the gleaming curls that rested against her cheek. It was the sort of gesture he might have made if confronted by a well groomed dog or a favourite horse, and she was too shocked to shrink away. She merely looked up at him, and as he met her eyes – unusually beautiful eyes in the flickering light of the candles – he smiled a little quizzically.

"You must permit me to observe that you make a very charming widow, Mrs Templeton. I am sure it should not be too difficult for you to secure a second husband, and I recommend strongly that you make such an acquisition your priority. The married state may not hold many attractions for you, but anything, I should think, would be preferable to your present life as an upper class servant. Lady Mapelforth may treat you quite generously, even with kindness and consideration, but she is still your employer, and she can order your life in any way she sees fit. You are at her beck and call, obliged to pay attention to all her wishes – as was made very plain this evening, when she obliged you to enter this room in my company, merely to search for a book. To all the other guests it was made perfectly obvious that the unusually personable Mrs Templeton was, despite the quality of her birth and upbringing, of no greater significance in this household than the butler or her ladyship's personal maid. . . rather less, in fact."

Fanny stared at him, and then she stepped back abruptly. "I can assure you," she said very distinctly, "that I am not interested in looking for another husband. I feel very comfortable in this house, and Lady Mapelforth is extremely good to me. In fact, she treats me as if I were her own daughter. And when - when she asked me to join you in this room, she was merely attempting to be helpful."

"Indeed!" He was standing very still, and watching her attentively. "In what way?"

"She knew how anxious I was about Justine, and that I wanted – needed – to speak with you. To ask if you might, after all, be prepared to help."

"Ah! I understand! Her ladyship felt that, brutish ogre as I am, I might still be persuaded to show a little compassion. If approached by a beautiful young woman, I might somehow or other be induced to remember that my tragic younger brother and his enchanting wife were being allowed to starve in the gutter."

She couldn't answer him, and he smiled unpleasantly at her downcast face.

"I am astonished that a woman like Lady Mapelforth should have allowed herself to become involved in such a scheme. I should have thought she would be much too concerned about the risks to her position. You must indeed be a persuasive little minx." He strode towards the door. "Pray inform her ladyship that my enthusiasm for the Persian wars has quite abated. Also, that I have just now recollected an urgent engagement elsewhere. It is distressing when such a situation arises, but I'm sure she will understand."

As if she had suddenly woken up, Fanny hurried towards him.

"My lord . . . you're not leaving?"

"Certainly I am." As he looked straight at her, she could see that his face was a mask of icy rage. "And Mrs Templeton, if we should meet again in any kind of public place, I trust you will not seek to take advantage of our fragile kinship. Some of my male friends are quite easily seduced. But I daresay that possibility has occurred to you already."

Flinging the door open he strode out into the hall, where Caldicott was endeavouring to look as if he had heard nothing whatsoever of this final outburst. Having asked for his cloak, hat and cane, he turned once more towards Fanny.

"Pray convey to Lady Mapelforth the pleasure I have derived from such a diverting evening. To say nothing, of course, of a very splendid dinner!"

Snatching his cloak from a footman he slung it round his own shoulders, then seized his hat and cane. More footmen stepped forward and the hall door opened, admitting the brisk chill of an October night.

When he had gone, Caldicott turned to look enquiringly in Fanny's direction. But she was already on the stairs, fleeing up to her room.

Seated on the stool in front of her dressing-table, she stared into the mirror with a kind of angry perplexity. *What had she done?* How could she have let her employer down so badly?

Then she absorbed the real meaning of Ordley's parting words. Her cheeks flushed painfully, but eventually the colour faded, leaving her very pale.

III

Told of the Marquis's premature departure, Lady Mapelforth was most displeased. When she discovered the precise circumstances, she was outraged and appalled. Simply because of Fanny's ridiculous anxiety, she had agreed that his lordship should be waylaid under her roof, had even assisted with the waylaying. But Fanny had promised, had given her word that Lord Ordley should not be embarrassed or made uncomfortable. And now this. . . . What must the Marquis think of her? What was going to be said about her hospitality?

For at least a couple of days things got worse rather than better, but then gradually it became clear to her that nobody actually knew about Lord Ordley's discomfiture, or his annoyance. Since he was unmarried there was no lady to exercise a baleful influence on his behalf – and he, it appeared, had gone back to his regiment.

Perhaps, in the end, there had not been much harm done. He was a charming man, though, and she must always regret the loss of his acquaintance. Fanny had better not think of doing such a thing again.

Fanny was very sorry to have displeased her employer and briefly it did occur to her that she might be about to lose her situation, but it wasn't long before the storm abated.

She didn't have enough money to hire a chaise and in any case it was hardly the moment to seek further indulgence from Lady Mapelforth, but this scarcely mattered because she had little reason, now, to disturb herself about the well being of

Justine. A searching letter, despatched the day after her own meeting with Lord Ordley, had produced a reply that was almost disarming in its honesty.

Justine was very sorry her stepmother had not properly understood – she was quite certain that in her last letter she had made it plain how much their circumstances had altered. There was no longer the least need for anxiety to be felt on her account. Darling Freddie's leg was mending so rapidly that he could now hobble about without so much as a stick to support him, and their new surroundings were such that she no longer found her situation in the least irksome. His lordship had whisked them away from that dreadful apartment in Bath and established them in the prettiest, most comfortable little house. He had supplied them with sufficient funds to see them through the confinement, and – more than that – had promised Freddie an exceedingly generous allowance. On top of everything, he had also promised them a house many sizes larger than Rose Lodge, just as soon as it could be got ready for them. The Dower House, two miles from Whitcombe Park, had until very recently been the home of Freddie's mamma, the Dowager Marchioness, but now that she had removed to that great big place in Bath it was not wanted any more, and would be perfect for her and Freddie.

Justine ran on, through several sheets of rose-pink paper, about all the other advantages that had recently been showered upon them. A daily supply of fruit and vegetables from the estate, not to mention poultry and game, rabbits, etcetera. And of course there was nothing for her to do, for they already had a cook, a housemaid and a manservant, and very soon there would be a nursemaid arriving from Bath. Freddie had always said that his brother would come up trumps in the end, and he had been very right. She could not say how grateful they both were to his lordship, who was undoubtedly a most generous man. It was simply so regrettable that Fanny had misread – or perhaps had not received? – her last few letters.

The Marquis certainly appeared to have treated his brother

and sister-in-law with the most remarkable degree of generosity, and Fanny was very happy for them. She was also intensely relieved. From her own point of view, she hoped she would never again be obliged to face the insolence in his lordship's cold black eyes. But she also wished, very profoundly, that she had not so seriously misjudged him.

Why, oh why had he not acknowledged at least some of her letters?

Fanny placed her stepdaughter's latest communication in front of her employer – on her breakfast tray, in point of fact – and waited a little apprehensively for her response, which was not long in coming.

"Well, well! Did I not tell you the girl was entirely without scruple? My advice to you now, my dear Fanny, is that you put her completely out of your head, at any rate for the time being. I feel, though, that you should write an apology to Lord Ordley. I am quite sure the poor man deserves it."

Fanny did not send any apology to the Marquis of Ordley; but she did complete a couple of lawn nightgowns for the baby, despatching them to Whitcombe in company with several yards of the finest satin ribbon.

When November came, she and Lady Mapelforth were still in London. Reluctant to part from the comforts of Clarges Street, her ladyship lingered until the last of her friends had left for the country, then she developed a cold. As the cold turned to a bronchial infection her doctor warned that the smoke-filled streets were doing her no good, and as soon as she was fit for the journey they travelled into Dorset, where she had been invited to spend the winter with relations who lived near Shaftesbury.

Despite black winter woods and frost-rimed hedgerows Fanny enjoyed the Dorset countryside, and her walks with Pug, but after a few weeks Lady Mapelforth was bored to distraction and in December she developed another bad cold. As snow began to fall heavily, the doctor from Shaftesbury declared himself concerned about her ladyship.

Fanny was also concerned and for much of the time she

remained with her employer, re-arranging pillows, reading aloud, even helping Florence to ease her ladyship's sizeable form in and out of bed. Then January came, and a pale sun began to melt the snow. Lady Mapelforth received letters telling her that a number of friends were once again in London, and her spirits lifted. Soon the doctor was able to declare his patient fully recovered, and on the fifteenth day of January, attended by Fanny, Pug and the indispensable Florence, her ladyship set out upon the London road.

In town she was greeted by her brother and by a stream of visitors. Most brought a considerable amount of gossip, and several showed a gratifying degree of concern regarding her recent indisposition. Then the Vicomtesse de Sèvignes arrived.

Madame de Sèvignes had been exiled in London ever since her husband's execution twenty years before and she had no intention, now, of returning to France. But she had relations who were over there, and from time to time they sent her news concerning her late husband's estates. One of the houses, a small château near Lyons, had long ago been burned by an angry mob; the other - as she had told her friend on many previous occasions – was still intact and being looked after by loyal and competent retainers. It was the most beautiful place, close to the sea and surrounded by flowers and vineyards, but although some members of her family occasionally stayed there, most of the time it was empty. The surrounding land was still magnificently productive – oranges, pomegranates, grapes and nectarines grew there in abundance, and then the vegetables were of a flavour quite unbelievable. The sweetest *poulets*, too, and one would never taste such veal. . . . if she were to arrive there, Lady Mapelforth would feel that she had been transported into paradise.

Fanny was never certain whether it was the flowers, the veal or the mention of paradise that finally settled things, but within hours Lady Mapelforth had made up her mind. They would be leaving for the South of France as soon as all appropriate arrangements could be made. It was quite safe, now, to travel abroad – even Lord Ordley had told them it would be safe enough after Christmas, had he not? - and only think what an adventure they would have. Her brother might express a little concern, but only a little. The truth was, he would like nothing better than to spend every day at his club.

Fanny was fond of her employer, and she understood that during the past winter the older woman had been sick and frightened. Now she longed for a little warmth, colour and diversion, and it was Fanny's duty to see that the expedition was made as comfortable as possible.

Justine's confinement was approaching fast, but she was well looked after and Fanny no longer felt any particular sense of responsibility where she was concerned. With the help of a Frenchman who was nearly related to the Vicomtesse, various arrangements were made swiftly and within a very short time they found themselves setting out for the continent.

IV

Light winds made their crossing swift and smooth, and when
they reached Calais just before dusk all the party was still in
excellent spirits. On the crowded quayside they were met by
noise, stench and some incivility, but such things were occasionally
to be found in England, and as Fanny spoke quite a lot of French
it wasn't long before they found the carriage that had been
arranged to meet them. It had been recommended that they
should not stay the night in Calais, and though this was irksome
it did mean they would be wasting very little time. They were to
halt just a few miles away, at a respectable inn in the village of
Manchette, and as Lady Mapelforth entered the well appointed
carriage she declared herself quite satisfied with the way things
were going. In the end Caldicott had been left behind, but
Fanny, Pug and Florence joined her inside, and John the footman
climbed up to take his place beside a swarthy French coachman.
Tall and muscular, John carried a pistol and knew very well how
to use it. Very firmly, Lady Mapelforth had declined to engage
French out-riders, but she would have felt a great deal less
happy if they had not been able to take John with them.

As they set off Fanny felt uneasy, partly because she was sure
things could not continue to go quite so smoothly; and within a
fairly short time she had been proved right.

The inn at Manchette turned out to be cramped and dirty,
with just one available bedchamber. Among the inn's roughly
made furnishings there was hardly one chair on which it would
have been safe for Lady Mapelforth to sit down, and a single

glance at the bedding convinced her that she would not be taking her clothes off that night. Dinner turned out to be a little better – the soup, at least, was palatable – but when at last she retired to sleep her ladyship lay down fully clothed, at the same time pointing out that Fanny had better join her, since she could scarcely use either of the straw palliasses that had been tossed on to the floor. Florence must make shift to sleep on one, if she could manage it - at least, mercifully, they had not forgotten to bring Pug's velvet lined basket.

Astonishingly Lady Mapelforth appeared to sleep very well indeed, but when morning came they were confronted by coarse bread and bitter coffee and during the gruelling day that followed Fanny at least wished more than once that they had never set out. The next inn proved to be slightly worse than the hostelry at Manchette, and so it went on. . . and on. As they rattled deeper into France, it occurred to Fanny that one often read about journeys of this sort, only nothing written in a book could adequately describe the horrors involved. Every inn was dirty, every road in an appalling condition and – perhaps not surprisingly – most of the faces they encountered were hostile

Miraculously, though, Lady Mapelforth's energy and fortitude seemed more than equal to the demands being made, and if anything she became increasingly cheerful. Having asked a surly French landlord to hold Pug while she descended from her carriage, she was not pleased to see the wretched man drop his burden on to a pile of manure; but she remained undaunted. While onlookers laughed uproariously she directed an icy glare at the landlord, then asked John to place poor Pug under the stableyard pump. After which she gathered her skirts and stalked into the inn as if she were arriving at the Assembly Rooms in Bath.

Florence feared they might encounter footpads, or even something worse. Jules – the coachman - might quite possibly be in the pay of some powerful robber, and on one occasion Florence was ready to swear that they were being followed. When she held her head in a certain position she could quite definitely, she said, hear the sound of other hooves. They were always a little distance behind, and she was sure they were being held back, just out of sight.

Very sensibly Lady Mapelforth ordered the carriage to stop while John went back to investigate whoever it was who was pursuing them, but nothing was found. Apparently the whole thing had come out of Florence's nervous imagination, and before they moved forward again she was obliged to endure a sharp rebuke from her employer.

When they had been on the road for ten or twelve days the air began to get noticeably warmer, and the clouds dissipated. A week after that they came to a high ridge, and when the horses had been dragging up hill for almost an hour they suddenly saw in front of them the dark blue line of the Mediterranean sea. A light, sweet scent came drifting to meet them, and Lady Mapelforth declared that it was mimosa. She had smelt it in Italy, when she was quite a girl, and had never forgotten.

For the past few days they had been travelling through country that was better managed than anything they had so far seen in France, and when not long afterwards they came to the Maison Sèvignes they found its gates freshly painted and standing wide to receive them. The Maison was a pretty, white-walled villa built in the style of a Roman pavilion, and though some of its curtains and carpets were shabby it was, on the whole, comfortable and very well furnished. The remaining servants appeared to have looked after it well, and they quickly made the English visitors comfortable. Within a day or so Fanny and her employer had recovered completely from the stresses of their journey, and even Florence declared the southern part of France to be 'not so very bad as she had thought it must be'.

There was a wonderful softness about the climate, and soon they were spending a great deal of time on the stone terrace in front of the villa. Lady Mapelforth's health seemed to have been restored completely, and Fanny was profoundly relieved. They had left England carrying a great quantity of varied medicaments, and now it seemed that hardly any of these were likely to be needed.

Lady Mapelforth declared that never in her life had she felt so completely at peace. Never, certainly, had she tasted such feathery omelettes or such delicious soups, and after a very few days she began to talk of carrying the two servants – the cook, anyway – back to England with her. Fanny did not imagine for a moment that either domestic could be induced to go, but it did not matter, for she understood quite well that her employer had no intention of attempting such a thing. She was simple expressing a kind of exuberance – relief because she was well again, and travelling in Europe.

They had been warned that there was not much society in the neighbourhood, but there was a good deal to see and after a few days they talked of planning a picnic. Marie might cook them a light, pleasant luncheon and Jacques could perhaps go with them, in case they should become lost.

But Fanny was beginning to realise that Jacques and his wife Marie had other things to think about. Every day men came to the rear entrance of the villa, hanging about in the yard and muttering, now and then glancing out to sea. If anything like a sail appeared they showed tremendous interest, but at other times they merely seemed to argue a lot, spreading their hands and gesticulating, apparently indifferent to the presence of foreigners. On impulse she warned John not to get involved with them, and he grinned sheepishly.

"Can't do nothin' else, ma'am. I don't know French, they don't talk no English."

The following morning, she decided to find out what was going on. Streaks of yellow sunlight were cutting cross the broad kitchen table, and Marie was kneading dough for the day's consignment of bread. When they had finished discussing menus, Fanny said:

"Marie, are the people here expecting a ship – a merchant vessel? Now that the war is over - "

Marie went on kneading for several seconds, then she looked up, staring blankly at Fanny.

"If it is not an impertinence, why do you ask, madame?"

Fanny almost laughed. "Because the men are always staring out to sea. I thought it might be fishing-boats they watch for. But there are no fishing-boats, are there?"

"No." Marie pushed a strand of black hair back from her face. She hesitated, then seemed to arrive at a decision. "We are looking for a ship, madame, but not for traders. We are watching for the Emperor."

"The Emperor. . . ?"

"He told us he would come back with the flowers, in the spring. So we watch."

"But your Emperor is on the island of Elba," Fanny said gently. "He cannot escape."

"He told us he would come back," Marie repeated firmly. "And now it is spring."

For the rest of the day Fanny was haunted by this. So much blind faith, pinned on one fallible man. There was the shadow of tragedy behind it, for they were doomed to terrible disappointment. Not that their disappointment was anything beside the consequences that would arise if they should ever prove to be right.

Eventually they had their picnic in a sheltered spot near the shore. The sun's heat was tempered by a sea breeze, and Marie's pâté tasted even better when sampled in the open air. They lingered for some time, and when they finally returned to the villa Lady Mapelforth went to rest upon her bed. Going to the kitchen to brew hot milk for her, Fanny found Marie seated at the kitchen table.

"Madame. . ." Abruptly, Marie stood up. "Jacques has said that there is something I should tell you."

Fanny felt an immediate tinge of anxiety. If Jacques and Marie were to leave, how would they know where to find adequate replacements? Isolated in such a place, what on earth would they do? But Marie had different things on her mind.

"Jacques believes you should know that our Emperor is coming back, and that it will not be safe for you to remain here."

Anxiety was replaced by relief, then by shock that these people should have allowed their obsession to take such a hold.

"Marie. . . ."

"The Emperor is coming, madame. *Vive l'Empereur.* I know, because Jacques has told me."

"You mean Napoleon Buonaparte has escaped?"

There was a look of exaltation in Marie's thin face. "The Emperor is free, and when he comes all our men will go with him, to march with the eagles. But you should go now, madame. It is not safe here, for you or for the other lady who is so much older."

Fanny drew a long breath. "I want to see Jacques."

"He has gone to Marseilles, but he will be back to-morrow."

When she took the warm milk up to Lady Mapelforth Fanny had no intention of passing on what she had just heard. After all, she hadn't spoken to Jacques yet. But Marie's words kept echoing in her mind. "*It is not safe. . . .*" If there should be any sort of truth in this wild rumour – and how was she to judge? – they would need to get away and back to England. And Lady Mapelforth had to be warned.

As calmly and lightly as possible, she passed on what Marie had told her. But far from flying into hysterics the older woman seemed to find the whole situation rather amusing.

"My poor girl, how can you believe such a ridiculous story? Napoleon escaped from Elba? You will be telling me next that King Louis the Sixteenth is alive, and is taking Marie Antoinette back to Versailles. Why in the world do you listen to such pitifully ignorant gossip? Surely you know that these backward people will make anything up?"

"I don't believe it is made up," Fanny said quietly. "There is truth in it, somewhere." She was remembering the faces of the men as they gazed out to sea, and her spine prickled. "Marie is not stupid, and I don't believe she lies. They have been told something."

"How?" Lady Mapelforth asked. "Has Buonaparte sent a

carrier pigeon – all the way from Elba?"

Fanny frowned. "I have asked to see Jacques," she admitted. "Today he has been in Marseilles, but he will be back in the morning."

"Good! Then he will see me also, and we will deal with this nonsense once and for all. *'March with the eagles. . . !'* Though I must say, if that were to be true it would certainly prove how little one can trust anyone in a country such as this."

When morning came it emerged that Jacques had already returned from Marseilles. Soon after breakfast Lady Mapelforth indicated that she was ready to receive him, and minutes later his presence was announced by a soft rap at the door. When he entered, bowing awkwardly and clasping a faded tricorne hat, he looked decidedly harassed.

"You wished to speak with me, madame?"

With the aid of her stick Lady Mapelforth indicated that he was to approach and stand directly in front of her, then she looked him directly in the eye and demanded to be told the truth.

"I do not wish to be deceived," she said firmly. "I want to know if you believe this absurd story to be true. . . if you are going to tell me that Napoleon Buonaparte has escaped from the island of Elba."

Her French was excellent when she wished it to be, and he clearly had no trouble in understanding her. For a moment he hesitated, then he bowed again.

"I know it to be true, madame. There are those who learn these things, and they do not lie. Our Emperor has broken free, and soon he will be in France. You should go, madame – you and the other lady, and your servants. Soon, all France will be on fire. You should go to-morrow. Your carriage is ready, and your coachman. His father once worked for Monsieur le Vicomte, and he will carry you safely."

Lady Mapelforth digested this. Fanny realised that she had received a shock, but she did a very good job of concealing the fact.

"And you?" She gestured in his direction. "Do you mean to welcome this murderer?"

Jacques' eyelids fluttered. He had not looked directly at either of them. "He is our Emperor, madame. Our father. . . the hope of France."

Lady Mapelforth threw him an acid look. "Well, my dear," turning to Fanny, "it appears this place is not so charming as we thought." To the Frenchman she added: "We shall leave to-morrow morning. Have the horses put to at sunrise."

When Florence was told she was hysterical for fifteen minutes, then it took more than an hour to complete the task of packing, but when Fanny did get to bed she slept soundly until wakened a little after first light.

V

When they drove away from the villa it was barely light. The sea was a dull grey and mist lay thick in the valleys, but the air was fresh and Fanny felt a sharp pang of regret as she looked back at what seemed to be a cake of sugar icing reflecting the last glimmer of starlight.

They travelled fast, shaking and rattling along rough roads, tilting alarmingly on the twists and bends of Provence. Determined not to show any regret Lady Mapelforth dozed for some time, making up for sleep lost during the night, while on the box John folded his arms around a loaded blunderbuss, and inside the carriage Florence held on to something else – under such conditions, Pug had a tendency to slide.

This was hard for them all, so soon after a gruelling journey from England, but there appeared to be little alternative, assuming that Jacques had not merely been relaying a fantasy without foundation.

After ten or twelve miles they stopped to change horses in a little village the other side of Cannes. Several men, Fanny noticed, were huddled in front of the inn, and over their heads a tattered tricolour had been nailed in place. As the horses were led away Jules got into conversation with one of the men, and before climbing back on to his box he paused to pass on what was being said.

"They have been told the Emperor Napoleon has sailed from Elba, in a ship that has been painted to look like an English frigate. They say he'll come ashore near Antibes, maybe today, maybe to-morrow."

Lady Mapelforth shrugged philosophically. "Well, we may be running away, which I do not like. But at least our reasons are sound."

They went on, wherever possible avoiding towns and even villages, frequently travelling after the fall of darkness, and every so often they heard scraps of news. Napoleon Buonaparte had landed, bringing with him a thousand men. . . . He was advancing towards Paris by the swifter Alpine route - which meant that he was not directly behind them – and the King, who was still in Paris, had sent troops out to meet him. Then two weeks later they learned that the troops had met with Buonaparte somewhere in the mountains, and had gone over to him 'as one man'. A few days after that they were told that the fortified town of Grenoble had opened its gates to him.

Eventually, Fanny and Lady Mapelforth drew near to Lyons. Forced by a damaged axle to enter the town, they discovered an excellent inn – the best Fanny had yet seen outside England - and decided to stay the night. The dinner was excellent, the linen clean, and when morning came mine host ventured to proffer some advice.

If the ladies were heading back to England, as he assumed they were, they should understand that every road to the Channel was now blocked. Not only English, but also many French people were desperate to leave the country, and places such as Dieppe and Calais hadn't a bed to spare. As for the ships, most were so crowded as to be unsafe and nearly all the private yachts – so he had been told – were now gone away. If they would heed his advice they would instead go north, into Belgium. All the Allied armies were assembling in the city of Bruxelles, and with them a great number of nobility.

Once there milady and her friend would be safe, and could plan to cross the Channel at their leisure. They had better drive straight through Paris - it would be a week or two yet before Napoleon reached the city, and if they were to go round through the country roads they might suffer a great deal of delay.

Lady Mapelforth found this suggestion enchanting. She had recently endured enough adventures to keep her friends amused throughout a whole season, but still she was not quite ready for a return to England, not when so much was happening. In Brussels they would have the benefit of good society, *and* the military to protect them.

Ten days later they reached Paris. Lady Mapelforth had hoped they might pause there, perhaps even for a day or so, but it was no longer a place in which to linger. The previous year's conflict had left some walls bullet-scarred – even blood stained – and though the squares and boulevards had an aura of elegance and civilisation much of the city was mired in filth, with shadowy side streets that spoke of nightmares. There was a dark excitement in the air, and from the way in which they glanced at foreigners it wasn't difficult to guess how parisians felt about the return of their Emperor. King Louis, it was said, was about to leave for London. After one uneasy night Lady Mapelforth called for her carriage – remarking, as she was helped aboard, that she had no great wish to see Paris ever again.

As swiftly as was decently possible they rolled through the streets and on to a north bound road, and within days they were well on the way to Brussels.

VI

Spring was hot and brilliant, and summer arrived within the first few days of May. In Brussels the parks filled up with muslin and parasols, and out in the level countryside picnic parties quickly became a common sight.

Five European nations had troops quartered in Brussels, and more were arriving every day, mainly from England. At the time of Napoleon's escape many British troops had been fighting in America and others had been temporarily at ease, with substantial numbers of officers either on leave or dwelling at home on half pay. For five years they had fought a desperate campaign against Boney, and in the end he had been thoroughly defeated. Who could have guessed – the Generals said – that in the end his captors would simply let him sail away?

Napoleon had reached Paris on the twentieth of March – two days after the departure of King Louis – and within hours had once again been in absolute control of France. He had the hearts and souls of the French nation, something no leader had managed before, and with them and many of his old generals behind him was likely to prove a formidable force.

If left alone he would soon be over-running his neighbours again, and in any case there was no doubt that he would always be a dangerous presence. He had to be defeated a second time, and in the free city of Brussels Europe's uneasy nations were now assembling their armies. From dawn until dusk marching feet and raucous bugles echoed through the town, colourful uniforms were everywhere and it might have seemed like one vast military camp, but for the fact that Society had also arrived, and in even more overwhelming numbers.

At first Europeans had flocked to Brussels because it seemed the safest place to be - short of actually crossing to England - but now it had also become the fashionable place to be. The Prince of Orange was there. The fugitive King Louis was in Ghent, but that was hardly a great distance away. In Brussels you could be part of the excitement, feel the anticipation, hear the rumours, then go and walk in the park, before returning to change for a glittering evening of balls and supper parties.

Arriving on the ninth of April, just one week after the great Duke of Wellington, Fanny and Lady Mapelforth had taken up temporary residence in the splendid Hotel du Parc, but although they were comfortable there it wasn't long before her ladyship decided she had to have a dwelling of her own. Brussels life appealed to her, and she had no intention of leaving so long as the present situation continued, so she took a small house in the rue d'Orsay, and began receiving as many friends as her pretty drawing-room would accommodate.

In the meantime, Fanny was not sure how she felt about all the excitement surrounding her. It was exhilarating and she enjoyed the colour and variety, in particular the rainbow assortment of nationalities, but she could not help being aware all the time of lurking, inescapable shadows.

Every time she saw a pretty girl laughing with a guardsman – blushing and fluttering her eyelashes - she thought about Napoleon Buonaparte and the vast army he was assembling. Soon now, as soon as he was ready, he would lead that army away from Paris and north towards the Belgian border, and then many of those brilliant uniforms would disappear like twigs in the grip of a forest fire, and what would happen then to the girls they had left behind?

When this thought was mentioned to Lady Mapelforth, she shrugged her shoulders and pointed out that life, after all, was an uncertain business at the best of times. Nobody could say how long any kind of happiness would last, and if some of these young women were about to lose the men they might have married – well, no doubt that was sad, but in years to come they would at least have memories. When they were older, such recollections might well prove a great deal more comfortable and charming than the husbands they would by that time have acquired.

Feeling that her employer might possibly be speaking from the heart, Fanny decided to say nothing more. She had never been in love – her own marriage had been a matter of friendship and convenience. But if a man she loved were to be lost in battle, in such circumstances. . . she did not believe she would be able to carry on.

Towards the end of April, her spirits were lifted by happy news from England. Justine had been delivered of a fine healthy son, and both were said to be doing well. Freddie, who broke the news, was clearly beside himself with happiness, the only shadow, as far as he was concerned, being the fact that he had not yet been able to re-join his regiment.

There were a number of fashionable shops in the town, and Lady Mapelforth lost no time in persuading Fanny to forsake the greys and mauves that proclaimed her widowhood. Such dowdiness, she said, was an embarrassment, particularly when every other woman was striving to look her best. There was a kind of ostentation, too, about constantly reminding people – whether or not they wished to know - that one had lost a husband.

Very much against her will she was fitted for a succession of elegant gowns, and to her further distress Lady Mapelforth insisted on paying for everything. When she was already in receipt of a generous salary this simply was not right, but protests merely caused her employer to shrug and remark that much more of this, and she would have another of her headaches. Quite apart from anything else, she would not allow Fanny to disgrace her.

On a warm afternoon in early June they went shopping again, this time for gloves and ribbons, and as they drove back through the old streets Fanny began to feel more relaxed. It was cool, in the narrow streets, and she loved the wonderful old buildings of the town. They passed the flower market, with its varied scents, and then they turned into the park, which they needed to cross, and at this point Lady Mapelforth became intrigued by an officer of obvious rank who was maintaining a position of sculptured rigidity, astride a black horse in the shelter of the trees.

It had been exceptionally warm that afternoon, and everything seemed to shimmer in the haze beneath the trees. Lady Mapelforth could not be quite sure that she was seeing aright. She lifted her lorgnette, then appealed to Fanny.

"Is that not the uniform of the Dragoons?" she enquired, directing her attention to the figure beneath the trees. "Or is it a Hussar. . . ? Yes, I do believe it is Hussar dress, but I am rather ignorant in these matters."

Fanny followed the direction of the pointing parasol, then despite the heat of the afternoon felt as if she were beginning to freeze. For she had no difficulty in identifying the figure. A blue coat, resplendent with scarlet facings and silver lace, a scarlet shako set rather low on the brow, a dark and brooding face. She would have known that face anywhere. And the Marquis of Ordley, she was well aware, was a colonel in the fifteenth Hussars.

At that precise moment he swung his horse around, and she saw that they had been recognised.

Lady Mapelforth gave an order to her coachman, and as the carriage came to a halt Lord Ordley rode alongside, saluting both ladies smartly.

"I am astonished, ma'am," he told Lady Mapelforth. And he certainly did look astonished, though his dark eyes rested on Fanny rather than her employer. "I had not the least idea that you had ventured so far. The last time we met it was in your own house, and I behaved shockingly. Having recollected an earlier engagement, I left without bidding you farewell or even offering my thanks for a most pleasant evening. Afterwards, I was appalled by the thought of my own conduct."

"Then you must no longer feel so." Overcome by Ordley's magnificence, her ladyship beamed at him. "Fanny conveyed your regrets to me, and I assure you that I understood."

He bowed. "I am deeply indebted to Mrs Templeton. But I give you my word, ma'am, if I had had the slightest idea you were in Brussels, I should have been seeking you out before this."

"We have been here for almost two months, sir."

"Two months?" Again his glance strayed towards Fanny, and this time she was certain there was a glint of mockery in his eyes. "I confess I can hardly believe it. Two months, and I had not the least idea. But I have been here only twenty-eight days."

Lady Mapelforth prepared to enjoy herself. "You will never believe the adventures we have had! Soon after Christmas Fanny and I crossed over into France, then we drove south to a place near Antibes. Well, it was quite charming, but the people were very odd – and scarcely had we arrived there when they told us Buonaparte had got away from his island, and was likely to land very near us. They told us we should go and I can assure you, sir, I needed little convincing. We travelled night and day until we got near Paris, then they said that the roads to Calais were all packed tight, and the boats, too. So we came here instead, and I was never more pleased about anything."

Lord Ordley seemed temporarily bereft of speech. He stared at Lady Mapelforth, then at Fanny. At last, he said:

"What can have possessed you?"

"Lady Mapelforth," Fanny told him quickly, "was very unwell last winter. Her doctors felt the Mediterranean air would be beneficial, and indeed it was. The villa was charming. And I don't believe we were ever in the slightest danger."

"Who went with you?" he asked curtly.

"My maid," Lady Mapelforth told him, "and one of my footmen, who is very reliable. Also our coachman – though, of course, he was a Frenchman – was extremely loyal and a great support to us. We could not have been more secure, I dare swear, if we had had three teams of out-riders."

Lord Ordley was silent for several seconds, then he shrugged. "Well, it seems that you came to no harm, and you both appear to be in excellent health." His eyes returning to Fanny, he added: "dangerous adventures evidently become you."

Lady Mapelforth was reminded of more pressing matters.

"My lord, what do you believe is going to happen? How long will it take us to be rid of that wretched man?"

"Napoleon Buonaparte? Who knows? It may take a little work, but in the end we shall be rid of him. Or at least he'll be placed somewhere more secure, where he can do the minimum of harm." He seemed to hesitate, very briefly. "Mrs Templeton, I was delighted to learn that your stepdaughter has been delivered of a boy."

"Yes. Yes, it's wonderful news." She had intended to speak stiffly, but the words did not come out quite as intended.

"Freddie says he is to be named after the Tsar Alexander. Your stepdaughter's idea, I think. She is not alone, though, a good many ladies are planning to inflict such things on their infants." He smiled. "The child's second name is to be Edward. My father's name and also your husband's, so I understand."

"I am pleased, as my husband would have been." She could not quite bring herself to smile in return. "I had not heard about the names."

Passers by jostled against Lord Ordley's horse, but he managed to maintain his place beside the carriage.

"I hope we shall all meet again soon." He appeared to be addressing Lady Mapelforth, but his eyes were still on Fanny.

The Dowager nodded affably. "So do I, sir. Perhaps you will be at the Maycrofts' supper, to-morrow evening."

"I don't recall, but perhaps I may. Next week, I think, there is something-or-other going on at the Richmonds' house. . . ."

"Her Grace's ball! Yes, indeed! I would not miss it for the world, and nor would Fanny. Even though she says she will not dance."

"Not dance?" The Colonel raised his eyebrows. "Freddie tells me that Mrs Templeton has been a widow for more than two years."

"Yes, well, Fanny is too proper about such things. Though I must own, I could wish such conduct were a little more common than it is these days."

"I'm sure you are right, ma'am, but a good many men may feel differently. I. . . I hope, Mrs Templeton, you will dance at the Duchess's ball. And if you do, that you will hold the waltz. I can claim near kinship, after all."

Fanny was too startled to reply, and before she could recover herself he had saluted and was backing away, his black charger stamping impatiently on the yellowing grass.

Lady Mapelforth instructed the coachman to drive on, and then she gave vent to her astonishment.

"Well, upon my word! It seems that his lordship means to strike a truce with you, Fanny. I must say, though, I think you should be a little careful. I never heard a word that would suggest Ordley is not to be trusted, but you are a widow, my dear, and quite poor. Many men might think it perfectly reasonable to regard you as fair game. You are not a young girl just out, and I'm sure you understand me."

Fanny did understand her. But she was not, because of that, going to hide away from the Richmonds' ball. Nor, she decided suddenly, was she going to eschew the dance floor. She would prove herself more than equal to the task of dealing with the Marquis of Ordley.

VII

As it turned out, Lord Ordley was present at the Maycrofts'
supper party. Not only that, but when they came to take their
places at the table it emerged that he had been placed beside
Fanny. As there were several titled women present – and Ordley
was the most important male guest – this was slightly surprising.
From Fanny's point of view, it was a decidedly uncomfortable
arrangement.

Through most of the first course his lordship maintained a
desultory conversation with the rather plump lady on his other
side, then suddenly he turned towards her.

"And so," he remarked softly, "my fears have proved groundless,
after all."

Her brows puckered.

"'Fears', my lord?"

"Yesterday I was half afraid you might prove to be some
sprite, conjured out of the afternoon heat. But here you are, an
enchanting creation of flesh and blood."

Fanny found his flirtatiousness annoying. Only a few months
earlier he had insulted and abused her, and she could not recall
that so far she had received any apology. No doubt she was
supposed to find his gallantry disarming, but in fact it struck her
as mildly repellent.

"As far as I am concerned, sir, you have no need to trouble
yourself with dinner-table politeness."

"Ah! Your pride was hurt, then, that evening in London."

"You behaved badly, my lord."

"Perhaps I did. But I was in the presence of a captivating woman, and in such circumstances we men do not always react as we should. As I recall, though, you managed the situation well." She felt his eyes on her. "And that is something else you do well."

"Something else?"

"You blush quite delightfully."

To Fanny's annoyance she felt the warmth in her cheeks deepen. Glancing across the table she encountered the admiring eyes of a young Guards officer, and firmly she looked down at the salmon escalope still lying untouched on her plate.

The Marquis said quietly: "You won't tell me you are unused to compliments. Poor Bradwell over there is plainly bowled over. He has no money, of course, but this place must be crawling with impressionable men, from penniless young cornets to firmly based merchants and nabobs, and a good many unattached, I daresay. They'll be in the very air you breathe, just waiting to snatch you up and bear you away to Elysian fields where everything you desire from life will be provided."

He leant a little closer. "You'll forgive me for pointing such things out to you, but we are nearly related, after all. Let me see. . . my brother is your stepson, and my new nephew is your grandson. We won't talk of that, though, for it's absurd, when you don't look a day more than twenty-three years old."

"I am twenty-six," she told him stiffly.

"Then I can give you ten years, for I am thirty-six. And yet you are my new sister's mamma!"

"It hardly matters." Taking a hasty sip from her hitherto untouched glass of champagne, she promptly choked. Tears rolled down her cheeks, and under cover of the tablecloth he handed her his immaculate linen handkerchief. Then he lifted the glass and placed it in her hand again.

"You should drink a little more. You are very intense."

"I am not intense." Dabbing at the tears, she added in a near whisper: "We have nothing to talk about, my lord. We should deal only with the weather. Or the war, perhaps."

"On the contrary, there is one matter I should very much like to discuss with you, only we need some privacy. I have been to this house two or three times, and I know there is a small apartment behind the drawing-room. . . after you have retired with the other ladies I will wait a few minutes, then follow you."

"Oh, no! Not another search for the Persian Wars!"

"That assignation was not my idea. Now, however – you will own there are things that should be discussed between us."

She looked directly at him. "Is it about Justine? Have you heard something. . . ?"

"Nothing, I imagine, that you don't know already, but we can't talk here. Already several pairs of eyes are observing us with curiosity."

The meal ran its long drawn out course. Lord Ordley was obliged to bestow a good deal of his attention elsewhere; together with the other officers present he was repeatedly subjected to questioning on military matters, and in any case he could hardly permit himself to neglect his other neighbour. When the ladies finally rose from the table he merely bowed in Fanny's direction, and as she left the room it seemed he might well have thought better of the proposed assignation.

In the drawing-room she drank a few sips of tea, then her employer disappeared in the direction of the card-room. Just for a moment she was quite alone, and almost without thinking she slipped out into the lobby. From the dining-room a muffled burst of laughter erupted, and it struck her that his lordship would find it fairly difficult to break away. Which, no doubt, was just as well. She turned back towards the drawing-room, but just as her fingers touched the door handle her arm was taken in a firm hold, and before she could say anything she was drawn away, through another door and into a small room where no more than four or five candles burned, and where they were quite alone.

The Marquis walked over to a long window, and drew the curtains back.

"This room," he said conversationally, "looks directly on to the park. On an evening such as this, one obtains an amazing view of the stars." He turned, and she saw the whiteness of his teeth as he smiled. "Don't be alarmed. It is quite unlikely that anyone will come to seek us out, and if they should do so they would not find our presence here in the least strange."

Fanny stared at him through the gloom. As he touched her arm she had felt an odd thrill of something very much like excitement. Now she had to remain very cool, and in command of herself.

"You mean," she remarked, "that you're very familiar with this house, and that you make a practice of bringing females into this room."

He shook his head at her. "What a suspicious little mind you have, Mrs Templeton. No, I do not normally inveigle women into this room, though I have been brought here for the purpose of discussing military matters with our host, Colonel Maycroft."

"Then if we are here to discuss something, perhaps you will tell me what it is. I imagine that it has to do with Justine – "

"Only in the sense that your stepdaughter was the reason for our original meeting. Mrs Templeton – " He broke off. "Please come and sit by the window. I am sure you know more of astronomy than I do. . . no doubt you'll be able to find Orion." When she didn't move, he sighed and shrugged his shoulders. "I beg your pardon. I brought you here so that I might apologise, possibly improve your opinion of me, and I'm making a pretty insufferable hand of it."

She stood very still. "Apologise?"

"You were gravely offended, were you not, that evening in London?"

"Yes. Yes, I was." She hesitated, and then she shrugged. "But I can understand that you were angry. Justifiably angry. You had already done more for your brother and Justine than anyone alive could have been expected to do, yet I had spoken as if they were being neglected." She walked across the room and seated herself beside the uncurtained window. "If you had not felt some resentment you would have been very nearly a saint."

He bent and lifted one of her hands, admiring the delicate shape of her finger-nails and the soft palm that was revealed when he turned it a little towards him. Very lightly, he kissed her fingers.

"You are an amazing woman," he said thoughtfully. "So beautiful, and so many other things as well. If I was rude to you, it was perhaps because I have always been wary of women. That is to say, I have been reluctant to take any woman as seriously as perhaps I should. And then, just yesterday, I saw you in the Park."

Fanny knew that she should draw her hand away, but couldn't bring herself to do so. She felt slightly dizzy, and wondered if this phenomenon might be the effect of champagne.

"You know," he went on, "that journey into the south of France was the most damnably imprudent thing I ever heard. Quite apart from any other consideration, with Buonaparte landing nearby you could have become involved in a great deal of unpleasantness. A beguiling little thing like you, and English to boot. . . ."

She interrupted him hastily.

"But we were never in any real danger, and I'm not particularly little. I'm five feet seven inches tall."

"With or without your shoes on?" glancing downwards at the dainty kid slippers peeping from beneath the hem of her gown. His fingers tightened on hers. "I am serious, however. Whatever your height, or other attributes, you must assure me that you will not let your employer compel you into any further adventures."

She laughed shakily. "There can hardly be any danger. Napoleon will not come so far as Brussels, and if we were to set out on any journey, from here, I'm sure Lady Mapelforth would be able to arrange any number of escorts."

There was a short silence, broken only by the sound of

hooves and carriage wheels, passing beyond the window.

"No," he said at last. "I'm sure there will be no danger. Except," more lightly, "that I and a few thousand other fellows may soon be ordered away to march up and down in front of the French. We may succeed in frightening them back to Paris, but it will be confoundedly boring, and it means that I have little time. Do you walk in the park?" he asked suddenly. "Early in the morning?"

"Sometimes."

"I ride there every morning, usually about seven o'clock. If you will come there to-morrow, I will leave my horse and we will visit the flower market."

"I love the flower market," she confessed rather breathlessly.

"Then seven o'clock. . . although I will wait for you until at least half past the hour."

VIII

On the way home Lady Mapelforth was in a state of elation because never before in her life had she enjoyed such a satisfactory evening at cards. Between them she and her partner had collected quite an enviable little pile of winnings, and she had decided that her share should be bestowed upon some form of charity. A new gown for Florence, and perhaps a pair of cuffs for their Belgian cook. Alternatively, she might invest in a collar and leash for Pug, perhaps something more ornamental than he was accustomed to wear.

"What do you say, my dear?" she asked Fanny happily. "Lady Frobisher's pug has a collar inset with emeralds. Only small stones, you understand, but most becoming. And he has a coat of quilted satin, which prevents him from taking another nasty cough like the one that ravaged him two seasons ago."

"I'm sure Pug would love a coat of quilted satin," Fanny heard herself reply.

Lady Mapelforth glanced at her with a touch of curiosity.

"I must say, my dear, I have never seen you in such looks as you were to-night. That very pale shade of yellow does suit you quite amazingly. I was somewhat surprised to find you placed next to our noble Marquis. . . I hope he did not behave too outrageously. No doubt he won't have done, in such company. I was sorry to lose sight of you after dinner, I did so want you to enjoy the evening. It might be a good idea, you know, if you were to take a hand of cards sometimes."

"Perhaps it might," Fanny agreed, hardly aware of what she

was saying. She was grappling with a sense of unreality. Nothing around her seemed to be as it had been only an hour or so before - her world had dissolved and re-shaped itself, so that now it centred on a pair of very dark eyes and a firm, masculine mouth that had taken to dropping kisses on her hands.

As she stared at the starlit heavens and felt the warm night wrapping her about, she felt that she was unlikely to sleep a wink before daybreak. But if she did sleep she would almost certainly meet again those eyes, and that hard jaw-line, and that crisp dark hair.

In the end Fanny did get a reasonable amount of sleep, and by six o'clock in the morning she was up and fully dressed. Sometimes Florence accompanied her when she went to the park with Pug, but Florence was not going to be involved in this morning's expedition. Fanny was not an unmarried girl, and anyway, at such an hour she was hardly likely to be observed by that many pairs of interested eyes.

When she set out the air was still reasonably fresh, and the early sunlight's hazy brilliance made her think of summer mornings in England. There were very few people about in the park, and at first she thought Lord Ordley had not yet made an appearance. After all, it was still not quite seven o'clock.

And then she saw him waiting under the trees, apparently unmoving on his big black horse.

Without any diffidence she walked on until she was standing almost under the horse's nose. As Ordley dismounted she looked up into his face, and the pleasure in his eyes took her breath away.

"You are on time!" he told her. As the Cathedral clock began to chime, he added: "I would have waited. But you are on time!" He took her gloved hand and saluted it, all the time gazing into her face. "I am sure," he went on, "you do not need me to tell you that you look adorable. You cannot have had much time for sleep, yet you are as fresh as a newly opened rose."

For some reason, Fanny did not feel in the slightest bit uncomfortable. "I had no idea," she remarked, "that soldiers were capable of such poetic language."

She put up a hand to touch the charger's neck, then caressed one of its ears. The Marquis, she sensed, stiffened warily, and a mounted trooper hovering nearby looked ready to call a warning. Resisting the temptation to drop a kiss on the creature's nose, Fanny turned aside with a smile in her eyes.

"I'm not frightened of horses," she told Lord Ordley. "All my life I've been accustomed to ride – at least, until the last few years."

"But Fedor is no lady's mount." He handed Fedor's reins to the trooper, and offered his arm to Fanny. "Now, let us walk to the flower market. Unless, of course, you find it boring?"

She shook her head. "I visit it quite often, but I could never find it boring." She added demurely: "Usually, I am accompanied by Lady Mapelforth's pug. He sadly needs the exercise."

"Well, whatever the requirements of her ladyship's lap-dog, I'm glad you didn't bring him today. We still have a lot to talk about, and I don't intend to share you. Incidentally, I hear that Lady Mapelforth had the most extraordinary success last night. I suspect she must have perfected the art of – shall we say, of managing the cards. I would not dream of suggesting her ladyship stoops to dishonourable practice."

Fanny smiled. "I'm very sure that Lady Mapelforth does nothing she would not personally consider to be honourable."

As he guided her across the road and into a maze of narrow streets she noticed how the peasant women stared at him. He was magnificent in his military dress, and normally she might have found it difficult to believe that anyone so astonishingly handsome could be walking through these streets because of her. At that moment, though, it didn't feel in the least strange.

"Do you realise," he asked suddenly, "how much time we have wasted? We have both been here in Brussels for weeks, and yet we met only two days ago. Why in the world could I not have been told you were coming here?"

"Surely you did not expect to be supplied with details of all our movements?"

"No. . . perhaps not. I should have employed a regiment of spies."

"Who would not, I'm afraid, have been very useful. Lady Mapelforth's plans are quite fluid, and are liable to be changed at very short notice. I think she has also become addicted to travel. When the excitement here has abated a little she may decide to visit Austria, or Italy, or somewhere like that. I would not like to make any kind of prediction concerning our next destination."

The Marquis frowned.

"But does this mean you must necessarily accompany her?"

"I'm afraid it does."

A farm cart trundled past them, heavily laden with produce and weaving erratically. Gripping Fanny's arm, he whisked her out of the way.

"My – " He checked himself. "I'm sorry. We should not have come through these narrow streets."

She felt slightly shaky, but not from fear of the cart. "I walk through here all the time," she said. "I love the streets of Brussels."

"Until now," he confessed, "I have paid them scant attention. I believe, though, that I shall remember them with considerable fondness."

They were in the flower market, and besieged by early summer scents. Carts were still arriving, laden with blooms from the fields and gardens of Brabant, and abruptly Ordley moved to one of the stalls, turning back with an armful of crimson roses. Their scent was like incense, and as he placed them in Fanny's hands the female stall-holder watched with a knowing smile.

"*Madame est très belle,*" she remarked. "*Elle est charmante.*"

"She is," he agreed, and handed the woman an additional coin. "I would have preferred pink roses," he told Fanny. "To me, you are more like a pink rose. On this occasion, however. . . ."

She could not think of a thing to say, but in her eyes he saw something that made him think of clear green water, just touched by sunlight. He guided her through the market, and back into the quiet streets from which they had emerged.

"During these next few days," he said suddenly, "I shall be very much occupied, which means that we may not meet again until the fifteenth. You will be at the Richmonds' house, will you not?"

"Yes. . . yes. I am sure Lady Mapelforth will not wish to miss the Duchess's ball."

"I hope you will not miss it. Also, that you will reserve every dance for me."

Feeling that she was walking on air rather than hard, cobbled streets, Fanny protested. "My lord, you cannot possibly dance only with one woman."

"Can I not?" He halted in the shadow of an ancient archway. "If it were not for this wretched war – or confrontation, or whatever you like to call it – there are things I would say to you, Fanny. I don't know how you might respond to them, but they could mean that I should be able to devote every free moment of my time to you, and no-one would be entitled to think it strange. Just for the moment Buonaparte's army stands between us like a cloud shutting out the sun, but it won't be there for long, I promise you. All I ask is that you take the greatest possible care of yourself, at all times, and don't allow Lady Mapelforth to rule your life. If it should become necessary, you must stand up to her and defy her."

Standing beside him with her arms full of roses, Fanny looked up into his face. In her eyes, there was no shadow of pretence. At the same time, she shook her head.

"I assure you, my lord, she is not a martinet. Indeed, she has been a very good friend to me."

"Very well. But please try to make it 'Edward'. Now. . ." They were entering the rue d'Orsay, and he paused again. "I shall not embarrass you by walking any further. Instead, I shall watch until you disappear from my sight. Then I shall continue to watch you, in my mind."

She smiled as she had never smiled at anyone in her life before, and he smiled back

"Take care of yourself, sweetheart. And thank you for this morning."

"Thank you for the roses."

There was no longer any excuse to linger, and five minutes later she was back inside Lady Mapelforth's house. So far her employer had not stirred outside her room, and without being noticed Fanny was able to arrange her roses in two handsome porcelain vases, one in the entrance lobby, another in the drawing-room. Keeping just two dark red buds for herself, she ran quickly up to her own room.

When Lady Mapelforth caught sight of the roses she not unnaturally assumed some kind friend must have sent them to her, and when Fanny confessed she had acquired them in the flower market her employer tut-tutted mildly.

But the reproof was delivered with an indulgent smile, and swiftly followed by the information that they were to dine that night with one of her oldest and dearest friends. In order to be fresh for the evening, they must both strive to get as much rest as possible during the heat of the day.

Which meant, Fanny realised, her employer would be playing cards again. And Pug, no doubt, would soon be acquiring a Dresden china water bowl.

IX

On the fifteenth day of June Brussels lay inert under a brazen sun, and most of the Richmonds' female guests spent much of the afternoon resting on their beds, but with the first cool breath of evening a hum of preparation began, particularly in those houses that clustered round the park, and as bells clanged ladies' maids scurried and carriages were put into readiness. In some quarters it was being observed that a grand ball was scarcely fitting.

According to new reports, Napoleon Buonaparte had now left Paris at the head of a large army and before very long would be well on his way to the Belgian frontier.

But then, the action ahead was unlikely to be more than a tidying-up operation. It was unfortunate that so many misguided Frenchmen should have flocked back to support the tattered eagle banners, but on the whole their reaction had been inevitable. This time, the Corsican Ogre would simply have to be removed once and for all, and Wellington, hero of the long Peninsular campaign, had arrived with the intention of doing just that. Everyone had faith in the Duke. Many of those men and women now crowding the city of Brussels would never have dreamt of being there, but for the fact that Wellington was about to deal with Napoleon, and they wanted to be in at the end.

If any conflict should develop it would probably turn out to be little more than a skirmish, and then the whole wretched business would be settled once and for all.

Even as the air began to cool, Fanny found that the slightest movement still brought a film of moisture to her forehead, and she resorted constantly to the Cologne bottle. She was in the habit of dressing quickly, but to-night she allowed Florence to do her hair and even to touch her lips with rouge. Her dress – for which Lady Mapelforth had insisted on paying the bill – was the colour of very pale, unripe peaches, too soft to fight with her hair but strong enough to glow a little when the candles were lit. Her employer had also insisted upon lending her a necklace of creamy pearls, and they lay against her skin as if they loved it.

Staring at her own reflection, Fanny felt mildly bewildered. She didn't look in the least like a widow, she didn't even look twenty-six years old. She looked like a very young girl who had not yet been properly kissed - and this was fairly appropriate, for her marriage to Giles Templeton had been no more than a matter of convenience. He had needed someone to take charge of his daughter and she had needed a home. It had been as unromantic as that, and yet somehow it had worked. Their friendship had lasted until his death, and when he was no longer there she had felt bereft

"Oh, ma'am!" Florence's voice interrupted her thoughts. "You look so *beautiful. . .* and you going to a great ball. I reckon you might run off with any gentleman you fancied the look of!"

Fanny laughed, but it was a nervous laugh. Half unconsciously, she glanced towards the drawer where her faded crimson rosebuds were kept. What she felt for Lord Ordley – what he appeared to feel for her – was unreal, surely. On his side it might very likely melt away the very next time they met. On her side, though, it might linger. Perhaps for the rest of her life.

Lady Mapelforth had spent more than an hour trying to decide between two expensive additions to her own wardrobe, and when Fanny joined her she was still unable to make up her mind. There was a puce-coloured satin robe, to be worn with an over-dress of silver lace ornamented by silver bugles, and there was emerald green satin with gold bugles and an accompanying head-dress of black feathers. Asked for her opinion, Fanny took the cowardly way out, insisting that Lady Mapelforth really must make her own decision. After all, if she were not entirely happy with her own appearance she would hardly be able to enjoy the ball.

Faced with such a prospect, her ladyship decided in favour of emerald satin.

In the end, they set out rather late. To begin with Lady Mapelforth mislaid one of her favourite pendants, and a frantic search had to be conducted. After half an hour it was found, but by that time their elderly coachman had become confused about his orders and when the carriage finally drew to a halt outside it was very nearly nine o'clock. By fashionable standards this was a perfectly reasonable hour, but Lady Mapelforth had had time to become agitated, and when they finally started off she was in no very good humour.

In the rue de la Blanchisserie *flambeaux* blazed everywhere, and as they stepped out of their carriage the warm air around them was noisy with wheels and the rattle of hooves. Carriages were thick in the surrounding streets, and people thronged wherever they looked. Through the doors and windows of the Richmonds' house music drifted into the night, and pausing on the steps Fanny caught a taste of excitement.

The ballroom was alive with rose-pink colour, and its tall columns had been wreathed with ribbons and flowers. Chandeliers cast a flood of light on to the heads of guests, and banners of the allied armies had been arranged wherever it was possible to drape them.

There were many wonderful gowns, Fanny noticed, and some of the young girls looked enchanting. There were also a considerable number of imposing dowagers and trim civilian gentlemen. But everything – and everybody – was cast into shadow by the brilliance of the uniforms. . . British, Dutch, Belgian and Prussian regiments were all represented, and in addition there was the court dress of those in attendance on the Prince of Orange. It was quite plain that everybody – of any significance – was present, but because the crush was so tremendous it was difficult to see who was there and who was not, and after speaking to one or two friends Lady Mapelforth became exasperated.

"This is hopeless," she complained. "They say the Duke is here, and his entourage, but a few of the officers seem to have rushed away. There has been some news of that wretched Napoleon."

"News?"

"Nothing of any importance, I'm sure, but military men love to be in a dash all the time." She looked faintly uncomfortable. "I am going to the card-room, Fanny. Lady Branwell and her cousin have urged me. You must go to sit with the Stevensons. I'm quite sure you will have a perfectly charming evening – you are a widow, after all, not a silly young girl. And if you do not see me again before supper, I am sure there will be any number of men delighted to lead you in."

She disappeared into the crush and Fanny drew back, so that she was standing close to the wall. Something had happened, was happening, she could tell. There was tension in the air, and on some of the faces around her. A number of young officers were dancing and on the whole they looked carefree enough, but there was a feeling. . . a sense of something. A young girl whirled past, and as she spun around Fanny saw that her face was as white as her dress.

"And did you think it so important to be fashionably late?"

Fanny turned, and with a sensation of exquisite relief found herself face to face with Edward Ordley.

"I beg your pardon." He sounded contrite. "But I was beginning to be afraid I wouldn't see you at all. I felt that the fates were conspiring against me, and I didn't know what to do."

She explained a few of the circumstances that had caused her to be late, but for once he didn't really appear to be listening. He led her to where a couple of chairs had been placed in an alcove, and when she was seated took his place beside her. Lifting one of her hands he deprived it of its pale glove, then carried the fingers up to his lips.

"My love. . . . I always thought you beautiful, but to-night I could go on gazing and never ask for anything more. No, no, that's a lie." He stared into her face. "The truth is, I don't know what I am saying."

She had almost forgotten the ominous tension surrounding them, but now it began closing in again.

"Something has happened," she said quietly. "Hasn't it?"

"Yes. There are reports which suggest that Buonaparte has crossed the Sambre river, outflanking the Prussians and heading towards us faster than was expected. It means that we must lose no time in going to meet him."

"So. . . when you thought you might not see me at all - "

"I had good reason." He was holding her hand very tightly, so tightly that she felt real pain. "I don't wish to alarm you, but it may be that you will have to leave Brussels, and if that situation should arise. . . . I want you to understand that you must lose no time, you mustn't hesitate. Don't let that ridiculous old woman talk you into remaining, simply because she does not believe there is any risk and doesn't wish to be inconvenienced."

"But you have always said there is not likely to be any real trouble."

"There may not be any real trouble, but we must not overlook such a possibility. Fanny, we know that Buonaparte is moving towards us at the head of a large army. Within just a few hours the entire Allied force will stand between him and this city, and I would almost be prepared to swear that you are in no danger. But I say 'almost', because in such cases there is always a risk, and I must be sure you are safe. If you should need to know, at any time, how things stand it will be best for you to ask Lady Charlotte Greville. Because of her connections she is always likely to have sound knowledge of what is happening. And if it's the case that your employer is refusing to leave, Lady Charlotte will be certain to know of people with whom you may travel. Before I forget. . . ." He pulled the gold signet ring from his little finger, and dropped it into her palm. "I want you to have this, not for sentimental reasons only, but because it could be of use to you with the authorities. If you are leaving and are able to make a choice, head for Antwerp. From there, you should quite easily find some means of reaching England."

Almost without the volition of her will, Fanny's fingers fastened round his ring.

"And you?" she asked, in a voice that was barely more than a whisper. "How shall I know. . . ?"

"You need not trouble about that. In the Service we know very well how to take care of ourselves."

She thought of the Peninsular War and its long catalogue of losses, of the cheerful young men who had never come home, and fear ran along her spine.

He was looking into her face, and by the light of candles flickering behind him she saw something in his eyes, a kind of pain that could have been anxiety.

"Don't you understand, Fanny? It is you, and you only I am thinking of. All will very likely go as merrily as a marriage bell, but in this life we cannot be certain of anything. I learned that a long time ago."

"And you leave Brussels – "

"I have orders to leave within the hour." He kissed her hand once more. "I daresay there is very little danger, and probably there was no need for you to be alarmed, but I could not take chances with your safety." He stood up and for a minute or two paced about the small alcove, while the sound of music reached them, and the odd burst of laughter. "We were to have had so many dances to-night," he said wryly, "and I can't tell you how much I was looking forward – and now I've got to leave you. . . my darling, dearest girl!" He moved to her and lifted her out of her chair, holding her in front of him without actually allowing his arms to encircle her. As she looked up at him her eyes were clouded with something like misery, but his were simply dark and opaque.

"Shall I take you to Lady Mapelforth?" he asked. "I don't like to leave you here alone."

She shook her head. "I'd rather you left me here."

Once again he kissed her hand, and then he walked away.

Clutching his signet ring she stood and watched him go, a tall figure in one of the most splendid uniforms conceived by man. She saw him disappear behind the trailing vines and showers of roses that guarded the entrance to the alcove, and when she could no longer distinguish the sound of his footsteps she moved out into the ballroom, to stand where he had found her. A dance had just ended, and the only sound was a rumble of subdued conversation. Once she saw the Duke of Wellington, moving through the crush at an easy pace, nodding here and there to an acquaintance. Then as he drew near to one of the doorways she saw that his pace quickened, and the officers surrounding him closed in a little.

She never did remember exactly what happened during the rest of that brilliant summer night, but she knew that large numbers of people soon started to take their leave from the house in the rue de la Blanchisserie. There was no panic but most of the officers left quickly, while all round the ballroom pretty young dancing partners and brides-to-be stood white-faced with families and friends. Wives hurried away to help their men with last minute arrangements, civilian gentlemen stepped outside to observe what was going on. Fanny stayed where she was for a while, then starting to feel noticeable went in search of Lady Mapelforth. Her ladyship was most annoyed to find that the ball was breaking up so early - her fellow card-players, even, had been drifting away in search of news, and just as she was enjoying a run of unbelievable luck. It was quite vexatious, and all because of that infuriating Frenchman, too. They had had him locked up securely, and why on earth had they let him go? Anyway, she really could not see why the military could not have postponed their activities until after the ball was over. But that, of course, was so very like the military.

As they waited for their carriage, Fanny heard one or two gentlemen talking casually of the 'skirmish' ahead. They seemed to feel the outcome was assured, and her spirits lifted a little, then sank again as she heard the sound of bugles and marching feet. The armies of Britain and her Allies were moving out to meet a hostile force – that was the reality, and no-one could predict how it was all going to end.

As they rattled through the streets towards the rue d'Orsay, Lady Mapelforth looked sideways at Fanny.

"Did you have your dance with Lord Ordley?" she asked. "I must say I never set eyes on him, but I remember that he asked you to reserve a dance. Did he not?"

"We didn't dance," Fanny said quietly.

"Well, I must may I'm very surprised. Maybe, of course, his duties didn't allow him to turn up for the ball, but I would have thought. . . ."

Whatever her thoughts were, though, she kept them to herself.

X

Back once more in their house by the park, Lady Mapelforth declared herself exhausted. A wide-eyed Florence - who had been watching several companies of infantrymen assemble at the end of the street – was summoned to assist her into bed, and Fanny went to her own room.

But there was to be little sleep for anyone that night. Drums and bugle calls filled the streets, backed by the sound of shouted commands and the jingle of accoutrements and at dawn Fanny was still sitting by her window. As the eastern sky began to brighten Sir Thomas Picton's Highlanders went by – hours before, at the Richmond ball, they had enlivened the earlier evening with their Highland dancing, and now they were marching away to war. Behind them stretched long columns of green-coated Riflemen, and behind the Riflemen crowds of bruxellois civilians.

The Highlanders and Riflemen marched on towards the Namur Gate, and giving way to sudden exhaustion Fanny went to lie on her bed. Edward Ordley's signet ring was tucked beneath the pillow, very close to her cheek, and its nearness gave her comfort. Standing alone in the ballroom a few hours earlier she had understood at last that Ordley's feeling for her was real. . . she had not been living in a fantasy. He loved her, perhaps as much - if that were possible - as she loved him.

She dropped into an uneasy doze, only to be woken by Florence, who had burst in fully clothed to say that she must come back to the window. All the soldiers were marching by, and they looked so beautiful, and there were banners and everything.

Fanny jumped up, feeling a sharp pang because Edward, on his black horse, might already have ridden past. Only later did she discover that the trumpets of the 15th Hussars had sounded To Horse before their Commander-in-Chief left the Richmonds' ball. Now, a few minutes before sunrise, Lord Ordley and his black charger were already several miles away along the dusty road to Nivelles.

She thrust back the shutters and opened her window, leaning out to see as much as she could, but by this time the pageant was thinning. Carts laden with fruit and vegetables were coming in from the country, and a handful of local tradespeople were making for their shops and bake-houses, but much of the Army had gone.

It was too late to sleep any more, and she dressed herself as quickly as possible. Staring at her own reflection in the handsome Flemish mirror that dominated her dressing-table, she noticed that her cheeks were very pale. That morning many women in Brussels would be looking much the same, but most would have their own comprehensible reasons. Fanny had reasons too, but because she did not want anyone to guess at them she allowed the helpful Florence to flick rouge on to her cheeks.

Sounds from outside drew her back to the window, and she saw that a group of officers were riding by. The Duke of Wellington and his staff had been awake for most of the night, but they showed no sign of tiredness as they moved at an easy pace towards the Namur Gate. If it had not been for their military dress, she thought, they might have been on their way to join a hunt, or to view some peaceful parade. As she leaned from the window she thought she heard the Duke laugh. The laugh was echoed, lightly and carelessly, then the little company's hoof-beats faded slowly into silence, and a brooding, unnatural tranquillity settled over Brussels.

Fanny went to see her employer, who was drinking hot chocolate and lamenting the fact that her sleep had been very seriously disturbed. She had been very much too tired to get out of her bed and stare at every company of Grenadiers that went by, but she had not been able to avoid hearing them and now she felt more exhausted than she had done before she went to bed.

The ball, she said, had been sadly mistimed. Had it been only a few days earlier everyone would have been free to enjoy themselves, and the evening would have been a great deal more comfortable.

"Last night," she remarked, "I talked to several gentlemen, and it was made clear to me that this fight against Napoleon will be won quite easily. Of course, I understand perfectly that Buonaparte is not very far away, and no doubt it will take a little time for Arthur Wellesley to deal with the matter. I am sure we shall hear many silly rumours, but we must not allow ourselves to become nervous. I for one shall remain in Brussels until all our young men are back. To do otherwise would be quite a scandal, besides being nonsensical. My only fear is that we may lack company."

This declaration came as a relief to Fanny, who had no intention of going anywhere until she knew what had happened to Edward Ordley. But she could only say:

"I think you are right, ma'am."

With the last of the troops gone, it was very quiet. When Fanny took Pug to the park she encountered one gentleman enjoying an early morning walk, and on the way back she met two bakers' carts and a cluster of chattering bruxelloises, but otherwise the town appeared strangely empty.

By twelve o'clock Lady Mapelforth had recovered enough to talk of visiting her dressmaker that afternoon, then just as she was beginning to think about luncheon they heard the sound of a light carriage approaching along the street. As it rolled to a halt outside their door, a servant rushed to answer the bell. When Fanny entered the drawing-room a moment or two later, she came face to face with Lady Palfrey and both her daughters.

XI

The Palfreys had been in Brussels for some weeks and they had all met on several occasions, but in Fanny's mind they would always be associated with a November evening in London. As Lady Palfrey was a close friend of her employer their sudden appearance did not surprise her particularly, but she was taken aback to find that the older Miss Palfrey was in floods of tears. She had obviously been crying for some time, and her swollen eyes were not being improved by the repeated use of a sodden handkerchief.

Lady Palfrey explained that poor Edwina had recently become engaged to Captain Denzil Maitland, who was an officer in the Dragoon Guards. They had met at Lady Mapelforth's house in London - just the previous November - but recently their friendship had developed, and there had been plans to make public an engagement.

"This very evening," Edwina put in, her voice choked.

"Yes, indeed, this very evening. But last night, when we got to the ball, poor Freddie had been sent away already. Edwina received a note from him, but it was no more than a few words. Nothing to tell her where his regiment was to be, or how long it would be before. . . . This morning we called upon Lady Charlotte, but she could not help, though she did promise to send us word so soon as she should have heard something."

Collapsing on to a sofa, Edwina put her head between her hands. Only a week or two earlier Fanny would have considered such a display undignified and unnecessary, but now she felt nothing but sympathy and when the sobs began again she sent for hartshorn, then for Madeira and wafer-thin biscuits. The hartshorn had a rallying effect upon Edwina, and her mother at least appeared to derive some comfort from the Madeira. After a time Lady Mapelforth appeared, and when the Palfreys eventually left they were all, quite noticeably, feeling more relaxed.

At the door, Fanny smiled at Edwina. "I am sure," she said, "everything is going to go well for Captain Maitland." And then she wished she had not said such a stupid thing

After the carriage had disappeared Fanny slipped upstairs to her own room, but almost immediately there was a knock on the door and Florence appeared, holding in her hand a letter that had just been delivered.

Fanny looked at the direction. She had seen that strong hand once only, but she would have known it anywhere. Immediately, she slit the letter open.

'My dear Fanny. . . .

'I am writing by the light of several candles, which have now begun to gutter. Just at this moment all is fairly quiet, and outside my window I can see the first flush of dawn. Having a few moments at my disposal, I should like to say what I wanted to say last night. What I should, perhaps, have said last night. We have had little time together, you and I, but it has been enough for me to know my mind, and I believe it has also been enough for you.

'When this wretched affair is over, you and I will be married. My dearest, we have a glorious future together. Until that future begins – always, eternally – you have my devoted love.'

Edward.

Fanny stood very still, staring at the letter, which barely seemed to be real. It contained everything she wanted from life, but she dared not dwell upon it. Not because Edward Ordley was likely to change his mind, but because –

There was a small mahogany box on her dressing-table. She had owned it for a long time, and had brought it from England because it contained one or two private things, among them a letter from her long dead father. She read Edward's letter once more, then she folded it and placed it in the mahogany box.

Lady Mapelforth had called for luncheon to be served at two o'clock, and although Fanny felt revolted by the mere thought of food she could not avoid joining her employer in the ornate dining-parlour. They sat down to a fricassée of chicken and almonds, followed by fresh fruit, and Lady Mapelforth was just reaching for a luscious peach when the windows started to rattle, and a long, menacing rumble set Pug yapping shrilly in his basket.

Lady Mapelforth dropped her peach.

"Well, of all the vexatious things! With all our troubles and anxieties, we might at least have been permitted to keep our fine weather. Now we are going to have a thunderstorm, and by to-morrow, I daresay, we shall not even be able to go out. It really is a great deal too bad."

Fanny got up and moved to the window. She was certain the fine weather had not yet broken and she was perfectly right, for outside the sun still shone and the sky was a clear, hard blue without sign of cloud. As she stood there the muffled roar came again, and this time the windows jumped in their frames. She spoke without looking round.

"I think," she said very slowly, "it is not thunder. I. . . believe it is the sound of gunfire."

Lady Mapelforth emitted a small shriek, and dropped her peach.

"Merciful Heavens! Then – in that case battle must have commenced."

"Yes," Fanny agreed, her throat dry. "It must have commenced."

Her stomach seemed to be in danger of falling through the floor, and she was finding it difficult to formulate words. But her agitation had nothing whatever to do with concern for her own safety, or even that of Lady Mapelforth. All she saw was a pair of eyes – dark, deep and inscrutable – and a handsome face beneath a scarlet shako.

Other sounds began to reach them – voices, running feet, the clatter of hooves – and Lady Mapelforth remarked that they were now about to suffer riots in the streets, but the reaction did not appear to last for long. Though the guns continued to rumble, Brussels was quiet again within half an hour. As if it were a normal afternoon some people went to walk in the park, others called upon their friends. Having decided against the dressmaker – for the time being, at any rate – Lady Mapelforth quickly began to feel restive, and it was a relief to her as well as to Fanny when a gentleman of their acquaintance arrived with information. Sober and middle-aged, Mr Felpersham had been – he confessed - a little discomposed, but he had recently heard some very encouraging news. The French, it seemed, had been engaged at a place called Charleroi, some twenty miles to the south of Brussels, and it was being said that they were now in full retreat. A tremendous victory appeared to have been won, and the great Duke was even now toasting the success of his armies.

The day before, Mr Felpersham said, he and his wife had been planning to leave for England, but now they felt quite differently about everything.

Fanny was too frightened to hope. She wanted to ask how their informant had come by his information, but could not bring the words out. When he had gone to spread his good news further she found that she was shaking, and was hugely relieved when her employer said they had better go to see Lady Charlotte. It was important, after all, to know the exact truth.

As they set out Florence helped Lady Mapelforth into the carriage, then she paused to say something that was clearly intended only for Fanny's ears.

"Ma'am. . . I went out in the town this morning."

"Yes?" Fanny replied a little absently.

"There was an old woman that spat in my face, and called me an English pig, and a fellow that talked about the Emperor getting back on his throne. Then that Gilles, that's one of our footmen, he told Robert the English was going to be massacred.

So Robert punched him, and now they've both got black eyes, ma'am."

Fanny frowned. "We are in a country very near to France, and there must be people who will wish to take the part of Napoleon. But I'm sure there are not many such people. Tell Robert he must not allow himself to be provoked."

"Yes, ma'am."

Fanny climbed into the carriage, and ten minutes later they were outside Lady Charlotte's door.

XII

Lady Charlotte's house was packed to the doors. While her employer advanced purposefully on an influential acquaintance – the wife of a Scottish General - Fanny found herself left near the drawing-room entrance, and as she studied the sober, anxious faces around her she decided Mr Felpersham's reassuring news did not appear to have had a wide impact.

She heard someone say they understood the situation to be confused, with much maneouvring around the dense forest of Soignes. Neither side, apparently, could be said to hold the ascendancy. The Army was widely spread out, and that was making it difficult for a powerful assault to be maintained.

Standing alone, twisting her fingers, Fanny wished she could find out more, but the dense crush made it difficult to move and the stifling heat was giving her a headache. Then an officer in a dust-stained green uniform walked towards her on his way to the door. Since they were slightly acquainted he acknowledged her, sketching a salute, and she seized her opportunity.

"I won't detain you, sir, but – but can you tell me how the battle is going?"

He stared at her abstractedly, and she noticed that his face was grey with fatigue and strain. "I wish I could tell you, Mrs Templeton, but the fact is that nobody knows yet how things may turn. Last night Boney came close to stealing a march on us. He came between us and the Prussians, and now it may be the devil's own work to hold him where he is. We had a brush with him today – at a place called Quatre-Bras, which is some twenty miles from here. We came off not too badly, but the Prussians had to endure their own encounter, and it's said they were driven back."

"Have there been many hurt?"

"The Highlanders took a hard beating, poor fellows. You are concerned for someone?"

It was impossible not to lie. "No. I just – it's so dreadful."

"I'll say one thing, ma'am. The Duke may well be obliged to fall back on Brussels, and if that happens it will be far from pleasant. A great many ladies and other civilians have left already, I believe. If I were to advise you, I would suggest that you go without delay."

When they were back in the carriage it emerged that Lady Mapelforth had been offered the very same advice, but - for the time being at any rate – she was firmly resolved to ignore it.

More and more battle-stained soldiers were now appearing in the streets, and as they turned a corner near the Namur Gate Fanny caught her first glimpse of a wagon full of wounded men. They appeared to have been thrown in, jumbled haphazardly, and she found the sight so shocking that she could not even bring herself to comment. For a few moments she thought she was going to disgrace herself by being physically sick, and her employer offered some crisp advice.

"Close your eyes, my dear, if you don't wish to look at things of that sort. At times such as this men get hurt, but it is not everyone, I believe, who can stand the sight."

The gunfire continued until past ten o'clock, then it ceased and there was an uneasy stillness, broken only by street noises and the periodic chiming of the Cathedral clock. But Brussels was not ready for sleep. Before supper a column of artillery had rumbled through, causing a good deal of panic. The uneasiness did not subside, and by midnight horses were being put to. A line of carriages rolled noisily through, heading towards Antwerp, and the activity did not stop.

After snatching an hour or so of sleep, Fanny woke at seven to find that Lady Mapelforth was calling for her. She found the older woman sitting up in bed, a cape around her shoulders, and it was obvious that she was upset. She had slept, she said, very badly. More importantly, she had recognised the fact that they were in a most unpleasant situation. At Lady Charlotte's house several people had advised her to leave Brussels without further delay, and she could see now how sound that advice had been. She had told Florence to begin packing immediately, and Fanny must make all other arrangements. They would need to be gone before noon, for Antwerp would be crowded and it might be increasingly hard to find places aboard any vessel bound for England.

This was not completely unexpected, but it was a shock. Fanny opened her mouth to protest, but was checked by her own conscience - Lady Mapelforth was considerably older than she was, and her health was not good. In any case, she had a perfect right to make decisions regarding her own safety. The problem was that Fanny could not imagine herself leaving without first finding out what had happened to Lord Ordley, and there was also the consideration that many ladies were now planning to help care for the wounded. If free to do so she would have liked to be one of them. . . somehow, she would have found the courage. Since her first duty was to Lady Mapelforth this was most unlikely to have been possible while her employer remained in Brussels, but she hated the thought of running away when so many were likely to be in need of help. Her mind was in turmoil, but for the moment she could only begin making preparations for departure.

Soon after eight o'clock a company of Belgian cavalry galloped into Brussels, apparently in full flight. Having told bystanders that all was lost and the French were at their heels, they charged through the town and on towards Ghent, leaving behind a trail of panic. There was no possibility of keeping this news from Lady Mapelforth, and after struggling for several minutes with an attack of palpitations her ladyship directed that they must leave within the hour. Robert was despatched to the stables - and then they were struck by a further blow. Their Belgian groom had gone, and with him the horses that had been purchased for the duration of their stay. Hasty enquiries revealed that the same thing had been happening across the city. . . those who had fled during the early hours had been fortunate, but after their departure grooms and stable lads had evidently decided to put their own interests first and hundreds of horses had been stolen. Some had been sold already, others – presumably - taken for sale elsewhere.

Lady Mapelforth descended into hysteria, and it was probably fortunate that Mr Felpersham decided it was his duty to call again. He had heard the shocking news, but he and his wife were fortunate because their English servant had been warned and had kept watch over the horses all night. It was, he said, quite untrue that the French were closing in – that had been a hum started by one company of frightened troops – but it was nevertheless time to be away, and this brought him to the main reason for his visit. There was going to be an empty seat in their carriage. They might fill it over and over again, of course, but as Lady Mapelforth and Mrs Templeton were alone, without any man to support them, he and Mrs Felpersham had thought of them before anyone else. The problem was, it was just one seat. Her ladyship's maid could go at the back with his wife's own girl, but for Mrs Templeton it would be necessary to make other arrangements.

Fanny interrupted, at this point, to say that it was not necessary to worry about her. She would be perfectly safe. Many other people would be staying on for a while at least, and it was possible she might be of use. Very soon, no doubt, someone would be kind enough to offer her a place and then she would be able to follow her employer.

But this was not accepted by Lady Mapelforth. No doubt Fanny would like to be a martyr, but there was absolutely no question of such a thing being allowed. There was certain to be someone who could squeeze her in and then they would all leave together, or more or less at the same time. Only after innumerable enquiries had been made did she reluctantly acknowledge the fact that something slightly different would have to be arranged. Sir John and Lady Coote, who were both of friends of hers, planned to set out the following day – they would not have chosen to delay, but a badly damaged axle made it impossible for them to leave earlier – and as they had a vacant seat they would be more than happy to take Mrs Templeton with them. It was the best that could be arranged, and from Fanny's point of view it was at least a short reprieve.

Since the Felpershams were to set out at three o'clock she arranged an early luncheon, and over cold duck washed down by Marsala the fugitive issued directions. Since Robert was leaving with his employer, Fanny and their two remaining Belgian maids must be sure to keep the doors securely locked. One or two of their friends might perhaps call with news or advice, but generally they must be most careful not to let anyone in. If Fanny should go out at all she must be extremely careful only to walk along the busiest thoroughfares. Really, though she would do better to stay within doors. It was not as though there were not things to be done. Some of their possessions were still to be packed up, and that would take her a little time - though, of course, all of their clothes were already tucked into the band-boxes which would be travelling with her ladyship. Fanny might keep a few necessities with her, but only the barest minimum, for what would happen if she were to depart in a very great hurry, with no time for loading baggage? The important thing was that she should be ready and waiting to leave the moment Sir John's carriage arrived.

"I shall await you in Antwerp," Lady Mapelforth stated, "for as long as I deem it to be safe, but if I do have to board the packet before you get there, you must be sure to seize the very next boat available." She looked faintly anxious. "You will. . . take *care* of yourself, won't you, my dear?"

"I shall be perfectly all right," Fanny assured her.

"Well, I do hope – but fortunately you are an extremely sensible young woman. That is something I recognised at the time of our very first meeting."

By now the fine weather had broken, and as the skies

blackened shafts of lightning began to break through. Thunder crashed overhead like the beginning of a celestial bombardment, and then the downpour started. Fanny shivered as she saw how quickly the gutters of Brussels became rivers of mud, and when she thought of all those men who were crawling back from Quatre Bras, battle stained and wounded – and those others being brought into the city in an endless stream of wagons and carts – a kind of nightmare descended on her.

For anyone about to start on a journey the conditions were hardly encouraging, but Lady Mapelforth was not tempted to waver. Tears coursed down her cheeks as she said good bye to Fanny, but she did not seem deterred by the storm. As she was fairly plump and the Felpershams' càrriage was smaller than her own it took some time to maneouvre her inside, but once settled she quickly fell into conversation with Mrs Felpersham, who was something of a kindred spirit. Protected by a large umbrella, Pug was handed up into the care of Florence, and the doors were shut. A hand waved from inside the carriage, and the vehicle began rolling forward along the muddy street.

Fanny smiled and waved, then she retreated inside. For a number of different reasons, she felt a sense of relief.

XIII

Fanny spent some going through the house, gathering up possessions that had been forgotten before her employer's departure. In Lady Mapelforth's room she discovered a flowery pink wrap and a pair of lemon kid gloves, in the little boudoir where she had so often sat to write her letters, Pug's basket was found sitting forlornly before the fireplace. Fanny packed the smaller oddments in a band-box, then took everything downstairs to await collection.

Alone in the drawing-room after supper, she spent some time watching the rain. For several days she had worn Edward's ring suspended from a chain around her neck. As the chain was long it had been tucked securely beneath the bosom of her dress, but now that she was alone she lifted it from its hiding-place, holding it tightly and wishing it could give her some sense of its owner's whereabouts. Then deeply tired she went to bed early and slept until dawn.

When she woke again, the rain had stopped and the sun was rising into a cloudless sky. After drinking a cup of chocolate she left the house and began making her way through the muddy streets, heading towards the Place Royale where many of the wounded were said to be assembled. It was Sunday, and outside every church worshippers overflowed into the streets. She saw injured men sitting in doorways and in the road; once, she saw a Highlander lying where he had apparently collapsed. In the Place Royale people were everywhere, Roman-Catholic Sisters in their starched coifs mingling with English gentlewomen, bruxellois physicians working side by side with Army doctors.

Steeling herself, she walked on until she came to an Englishwoman kneeling in the dirt, giving sips of water to a boy so smothered in mud that his uniform had become unrecognisable. She waited until the boy had stopped drinking, then she said:

"What can I do?"

The woman turned, and Fanny realised they were slightly acquainted.

"Dressings," she said. "They need bandages. If you go to the house over there, you'll be able to help."

Fanny spent the next few hours in a Flemish citizen's small front parlour, cutting up strips and squares of gauze and linen. The citizen's wife worked alongside her, but since she had little English they barely spoke. It was tedious work, and as the air grew warmer an almost unendurable stench rose from the streets outside, but Fanny knew she was fortunate by comparison with those tending upon wounded bodies.

Several times people came in to collect bandages, and usually they brought scraps of information. Most of the present injured had apparently been victims of Quatre-Bras or of some minor incident, but that would soon change and the numbers would increase, for after a sodden night the two armies had finally squared up to one another and battle had commenced. Napoleon and his forces were ranged upon high ground some twelve miles to the south of Brussels, while the Duke's armies faced them across a shallow valley, just two miles beyond the small village of Waterloo.

Naturally the entire British force would not be deployed at once, and some time after eleven o'clock reports still suggested that most of the cavalry had yet to be engaged, not that their turn wouldn't be certain to come soon. It would be madness to keep the Scots Greys, the Hussars and Dragoon Guards – not to mention the King's Own German Regiment – kicking their heels in the rear.

Bending over her work, Fanny wondered whether it might have been worse to wait in an English drawing-room, aware that she could not know anything until many hours after the whole affair was concluded. Or whether nothing could be harder than being, as she was, almost near enough to see the tragedy unfold.

Soon after one o'clock her companion disappeared, returning minutes later with cheese and bread, a bowl of peaches and a jug of red wine. She was a woman of about thirty, with pale, smooth hair tightly bound beneath a stiffened headdress, and a round face that seem inexhaustibly cheerful - until she stopped to gaze at something she had noticed outside the window, and Fanny saw that her eyes had filled with unshed tears.

Until the end of her life, Fanny thought, she would remember the woman, and the small, square room with its solid furnishings, and the blue and white bowl filled with peaches.

With many more wounded beginning to come in the demand for dressings was likely to increase, and Fanny worked on for several hours, until all at once she remembered Sir John Coote and the carriage that was to call for her at six o'clock. She had no intention whatsoever of leaving Brussels – if there had ever been any uncertainty in her mind, that had now dissipated – but she could not leave Sir John to hunt around the city in search of her. Also, she needed to make sure that Lady Mapelforth understood quite well where she was. Soon after half past five she handed her share of the bandage cutting to a newly arrived volunteer, and made her way back through the crowded streets. It was worse, much worse, than it had been, with carts full of wounded moving in long lines beneath the Namur Gate, and a number of bodies lying by the wayside. She hated walking past when there was so much to be done, but she would be back as quickly as she could possibly manage.

More people than ever were on their knees outside the churches, and she remembered how she had prayed that morning, inside the Flemish house.

Back in the rue d'Orsay their one remaining maid, Mariette, told her two ladies had called and asked her to say they would be going away out of Brussels that evening – only she could not remember their names. Nobody else had come, but she understood that very soon a carriage would be arriving to collect Madame Templeton. She had promised miladi that she would stay until Madame had gone, then she would leave herself and go quickly back to her village. Her mother had said she ought not to work in Bruxelles, and her mother had been very right.

Not wanting the girl to linger in an empty house, Fanny said that she could go immediately. Sir John and his carriage would be there very soon, and miladi would understand quite well. She would have said the same herself, if she had been there. Mariette was plainly grateful, and she certainly wasted no time. As Fanny went into the drawing-room to write a note, she heard a side door close and knew that she was alone.

She took up a pen, dipped it in the ink and began writing her note, which she had decided to leave fastened to the main entrance. She could hear a tall clock ticking solemnly in the hall, and also a vague cacophony of distant sound, but she was getting used to that. Because she was anxious and in a hurry, she dropped her pen and broke it. With much whirring and clanking, the hall clock began preparing to chime the hour, and she realised that it was four o'clock. Reaching for another pen she finished her note, in the process dropping spots of ink on the surface of the desk, and then the sound of wheels grinding to a halt on the cobbles outside brought her to her feet in one nervous movement. Someone began hammering on the door, and because there was no immediate response the hammering persisted, becoming more violent.

Fanny looked out of a window, and saw at once that the visitor was not Sir John Coote.

She went to the door and opened it cautiously, then was obliged to fling it wide as a tall young man in his twenties – or possibly younger - almost fell into the hall. His face was smoke-grimed and streaked with dust, and he was wearing a uniform that was torn and blood-spattered. Possibly as a result of fatigue his eyes seemed to be sunk deep in his head, and for a moment he leant against the door frame. Then he straightened, and made a visible effort to collect himself.

"Mrs Templeton. . . ?"

"Yes. . . . I am Mrs Templeton."

"Then will you please come with me? I was given orders to find you, and take you to Colonel the Marquis of Ordley. I. . . ." He swallowed. "I am Cornet Faraday. Ma'am, the Colonel is badly wounded, and there is no time to lose. Will you please come at once?"

XIV

For a few moments Fanny was aware of nothing, except that the world was spinning round her, then everything went black. When she came to herself she was seated on a chair and the young officer was bending over her, enquiring anxiously whether there was some restorative in the house.

"A little brandy would be the thing, if you have some," he suggested. "Or perhaps a glass of wine. I'm afraid you have had a shock, ma'am. I was not sufficiently discreet – "

"No, no." She was sitting upright, now. "You said – you said badly wounded. How badly?"

"The Colonel has more than one injury, but perhaps the worst thing is that he was left unattended for some time. His horse appears to have dragged him for some distance, until a bolt got the poor beast and it fell on top of him. When I left the surgeon was still with Lord Ordley. I think we should not waste any time, Mrs Templeton."

Fanny was never sure how she managed to overcome her terror and weakness, and jump to her feet. She asked him whether there was anything she should take with her. Linen for bandages – there were sheets in the house – perhaps towels? There were plenty of towels. And there was an unopened bottle of brandy in the dining parlour.

Perhaps Cornet Faraday would fetch the brandy, and while she went to collect the other things he might, perhaps, take a little himself. She found herself issuing directions as if she had been doing this sort of thing all her life, and he gazed at her admiringly.

"I was afraid," he confessed, "I was going to have a bit of bother when you passed out like that, but I see that I need not have worried. And thank you, ma'am, I will take a small glass of brandy. Wouldn't do to pass out myself, not when we've an eight mile drive ahead of us."

She wanted to ask whether he was fit to drive the vehicle – whatever it was – that awaited them outside in the street, but she realised there was no point. Someone had to drive it, and plainly enough he had come alone. Though there was blood on the sleeves of his coat, and on his breeches, she did not believe he had been hurt himself. Or at least she hoped not. She flew upstairs for the linen and towels and for her own cloak, then three or four minutes later she was back and Cornet Faraday had the door open.

To her surprise, the vehicle waiting outside was a smart and dashing cabriolet. Its wheels were picked out in yellow, and an unexpectedly fresh-looking grey stood between the shafts.

"Where did you get this?" she asked.

"Commandeered it," Cornet Faraday answered briefly.

As they drove out through the Namur Gate, Fanny woke to the fact that they were setting out on a nightmare. Since emerging from her fainting fit she had been feeling numb – mercifully numb – but as they rattled through the Gate her senses began to reel, and she clutched the side of the cabriolet.

The road was littered with up-turned carriages, and carts that were embedded deep in mud. Everywhere wounded men crawled on their hands and knees, while others lay dead or dying in pools of their own blood. There was mud and blood where the green verges had been, and the ripening corn was soaked with it. In the scattered woods pools of rain water glowed dark crimson, and the sun itself was sinking into a blood red haze.

Overhanging everything was the acrid odour of smoke, and the putrefying scent of corruption. Once she heard the long, sullen rumble of canon fire, not very far away.

Plainly Cornet Faraday was accustomed to driving fast

moving vehicles, and he negotiated every obstacle and morass with amazing facility. Seemingly indifferent to the sights and sounds around him, he concentrated all his attention on extracting as much speed as could possibly be managed from the game little horse. Now and again he enquired whether Fanny was all right, and sometimes he advised her to hold tight. Just once, he stopped to speak with another officer. The exchange lasted no more than a minute or so, and when it ended Faraday emitted what sounded like a whoop of exhilaration. Rattling on again, he shouted cheerfully:

"That's it, then! Boney's beat! The Guards finished it, and old Blucher's Prussians. . . . Hurrah!"

For the first time, Fanny realised that she had not once asked him about the battle. All those dead and broken bodies, that dark chaos had seemed like part of some natural disaster, some horrific event without hope of any positive outcome. If it was over, though, and Napoleon defeated, than that was wonderful. Or would have been, if it hadn't been for the bodies.

"When did it happen?" she asked abruptly. "I mean, Lord Ordley."

"When was he hurt? Whoa. . . . Hoy there, move aside, will you?" A group of weary Guardsmen edged out of their way, and Faraday glanced at Fanny. "The charge came soon after one o'clock. His lordship was in the van as he always is, and we were right on top of the gun crews. Heaven knows how many guns there were, but there was a solid line of'em, twelve pounders blazing away like fury. Our fellows were cut down like ripe wheat."

"And you were not hurt?" The question was mechanical, because she was trying to remember what she had been doing at one o'clock, when Edward Ordley was riding on to the guns.

"No, indeed. Devil's own luck." He went on: "The Colonel kept saying that you had to be fetched, then there was nothing for it but one of us must go to find you. We thought he was out of his head – delirious, you know – but the padre didn't agree."

"And was he conscious when you left?" Fanny asked with

difficulty.

"Lord, yes! Even when they had to operate he wouldn't let them knock him out. Just watched the whole thing without turning a hair."

They drove hard for more than an hour, then the vehicle swung left into a narrow track that ran between what appeared to be farm buildings. Emerging into a muddy expanse they turned again, and came to a halt. Climbing down, Faraday went to offer Fanny his hand.

"Take care how you step, ma'am. This place is an infernal mire."

Looking round, she saw that the only building of any size was a large stone barn. Two troopers were standing guard beside the barn's open door, and some kind of light was flickering through the dimness inside. Faraday came to stand at her elbow.

"You'd better let me take your arm," he offered. "Wouldn't want to twist your ankle, or anything like that."

The troopers saluted as they walked past, but Fanny didn't so much as glance in their direction.

She could see that the barn would normally have been stacked with hay or something of that sort, but just about everything seemed to have been removed, possibly by looting military. A lamp was glimmering in one corner, and beside it two men were standing. Between them, on a rough pallet, a third figure was stretched out.

Edward Ordley's coat and boots had been removed, and most of his body seemed to be swathed in bandages. Two or three rough blankets had been placed between him and the straw that covered the pallet. Fanny saw at once that he had noticed her, but as she hurried towards him one of the other men took a step forward. For the first time she noticed that he was wearing a kind of apron. And that the apron was stained with blood.

"Mrs Templeton?" He glanced at Faraday. "Well, well, come in, ma'am. I'm afraid you must have had a harrowing journey, but Lord Ordley said he was sure you'd undertake it. He is conscious, as you see, but a bit light-headed. Only to be expected, of course." He nodded towards the prostrate figure. "Here she is, my lord."

Fanny dropped on to her knees beside the Marquis, who was watching her with over-bright eyes.

"Edward. . . !" Her breath caught in her throat. "Thank Heaven you sent for me!"

"Of course I sent for you." The brilliant eyes smiled at her. "Don't look so cast down, Fanny. I am not so weak as I look. Anyway, I am still here. This. . . ." He indicated the tall figure who had greeted her. "This is Captain-Surgeon Arthur Sulimann. Known as Sully. And that excellent fellow," pointing to the second man, who had retreated a little, "that's Sam Bright. We have been together since. . . since Boney invited us all to the Peninsula."

His voice was stronger than she would have believed possible, but there was a hectic colour in his cheeks and she noticed that he remained very still. Then she saw that his unbandaged hand was inching its way towards her. Bright and the surgeon had retreated, and very gently she lifted the hand.

"I have been so worried," she murmured. "I heard what was happening, but I had no way of discovering where you were, or. . . . I thought we might never meet again."

"Instead of which you are here. And I am grateful."

"You cannot have imagined I would not come?"

"No. I knew very well that you would come, my beautiful red headed love. My anxiety was. . . there might be only a little time." As her tears spilt on to his hand, he closed his eyes. "You did receive my letter?"

"Yes. I could not believe that you had written to me, at a time when there must have been so many other things -"

"At such moments there are not many things a man feels truly obliged to deal with. I wanted to say my mind, so that you would understand and so that – " He winced visibly.

"What is it?" she asked.

"Nothing. Or very little. They've stitched me together in such a way – " He tried to move but abandoned the attempt, and

Captain Sulimann's voice came out of the shadows.

"Lord Ordley, I don't wish to interrupt you, but Mr Beresford is here."

"Beresford. . . ? Oh, yes. Good. He's a decent fellow. Said he would be back in time."

Looking up, Fanny saw a thin man in the dress of a clergyman, and a chill struck through her as it had at the Richmond ball.

Captain Sulimann leant towards her. "Madam, If you would step aside for a few moments, Mr Beresford would like to speak with you."

"With me?"

Feebly, Edward pressed her hand. "You may as well speak with him, Fanny. It's proper, I suppose. You have no friends here."

He closed his eyes, and turned his face away from her. Captain Sulimann was plainly exhausted and also short of time, but it was clear that he took a keen interest in his patient. He checked the bandages carefully, then placing a hand upon Edward's warm forehead asked if the pain were as severe as it had been.

"No," the Marquis responded unconvincingly.

"I think, sir, you would do well to try a few drops of laudanum. You would then get more rest."

"Damn you, Sully, I don't want any of your opiates. I need my wits – need to be awake. Mrs Templeton is here, you see. She has come."

The surgeon looked at Fanny.

"Indeed."

"So you see," Edward continued, "we can have the ceremony."

Fanny felt more frightened than she had ever felt in her life. Kneeling down again, she placed her fingers over his warm, dry hand.

"Edward, you should sleep a little. Perhaps the laudanum would help."

"How can I sleep when I am about to be married?"

She felt a sense of shock. Tears rose in her throat, and glancing at her face the surgeon bent closer to his patient.

"My lord, I believe we must steal Mrs Templeton away for a moment or two. Poor Beresford must talk a little about the ceremony, and he has not long to spare."

"Yes, yes." Edward Ordley closed his eyes. "Beresford must have his chat with Fanny. Only don't delay."

A few feet away they were joined by the padre, who looked grave.

"Madam. . . ." He cleared his throat. "I take it that you have no objection to being married in this way."

Fanny struggled to speak, but no words would come.

"I think," Captain Sulimann said gently, "you and Lord Ordley have an understanding, have you not?"

As they both stared at her, she gained control of herself.

"Two days ago," she confessed, "Lord Ordley wrote me a letter. In that letter he talked about marriage, but it was just before the battle at Quatre-Bras and I think – "

"Mrs Templeton, when a man offers marriage it can only be assumed that he knows what he is doing. Of course, if he is found to have been drunk at the time – but in this case that is unlikely. I have known the Colonel for some years, and I know his character. Certainly he appears most anxious to make you his wife."

Mr Beresford drew a watch from beneath his cassock. "The question is, ma'am, are you willing to proceed with this ceremony?"

"It seems so wrong. Captain Sulimann... as you said, he is light-headed."

The surgeon coughed, and put a finger down the tight-fitting neck of his uniform jacket.

"I think you do not need me to tell you that his lordship is a very sick man. Whether he will live or not, it is at this present beyond me to say. During the charge he received multiple wounds, and afterwards his mount dragged him for some considerable distance. Eventually, the poor beast was killed and collapsed on top of him. His right arm was all but severed by a sabre thrust, and though I believe we have managed to save that limb, there is always some danger. . . . Lord Ordley has, however, an excellent physique and there is a good possibility – though I ought not to put it more strongly – that he may be strong enough to overcome the whole and make a full recovery. I need hardly add that every care should be taken not to distress him, or to dampen his spirits needlessly."

"In such a situation," Mr Beresford put in, "I would be most reluctant to refuse the marriage rite, and it certainly appears to me that on this particular subject Lord Ordley's mind is clear enough."

There was a rough table beside them, and Fanny put out a hand so that she could lean on it for a moment. She was not going to faint. Not again. She thought of the strange little ceremony that had united her with Giles Templeton. Although that had taken place in a church amid benevolent friends, it had felt as if she and Giles were signing an agreement before an attorney.

The surgeon looked at her with concern. "Will you take a little brandy, ma'am?"

"No. Thank you, Captain Sulimann. You have been very honest with me, and I – I am grateful. But what if Lord Ordley should come to regret – "

Over her head the two men looked at one another.

"If that should prove to be the case," Mr Beresford told her, "then so long as the marriage is unconsummated, it can always be annulled. In the meanwhile, ma'am, you will have had the satisfaction of at least being his nurse. If, of course, you are prepared to undertake that task."

"I will look after him," she huskily. "I'll do everything possible. But will it really benefit him to know that I am his wife? Might it not become a source of anxiety? When the fever reduces, and he recalls what has been done?"

"Ma'am," Captain Sulimann said quietly, "I am very sure that he loves you. If you love him, you will have the answer to your question."

"I do, I do love him!" She put both hands up over her face, so that they should not see the tears that streamed from her eyes.

"Then let us not delay any longer."

Returning to Edward Ordley's side, she knelt down again beside him. He could see that she had been crying, for her eyes were red and the lashes wet, but as he looked at her there was a hint of hostility in his face.

"Well, what have you and Beresford and Sulimann been saying to one another? Have they talked you out of marrying me? Would it be such a dreadful thing, becoming my wife? Before the ink is dry on our marriage lines you could be free as air. Remember that, Fanny."

As his hot fingers reached for hers, she felt as if her heart were breaking. She placed a finger over his mouth, then bent and rested her own lips against a lock of dark hair which had somehow escaped the sinister bandage encircling his head.

"I am ready to marry you," she told him softly, "just as soon as your Chaplain is ready to open his prayer-book."

XV

Mr Beresford opened his battered prayer book some ten minutes later. As Captain Sulimann was needed elsewhere Sam Bright and Cornet Faraday had been appointed to act as witnesses, and despite his obvious weariness Faraday had proved useful in another way as well. It had occurred to him that they had no ring, and there could hardly be a marriage ritual without something to place on the bride's finger. Fanny produced Lord Ordley's signet, which still hung from its chain around her neck, but it was too big, and with some diffidence Faraday offered the ring he wore on his own little finger. It had been his grandmother's wedding ring – his grandfather had fought and died at Quebec, and for this reason he wore it as a token. As his fingers were somewhat thinner than Lord Ordley's it might solve the problem, and he would be honoured indeed if the Colonel would make use of it.

The ring was found to fit very well, and Fanny smiled gratefully at the young officer.

Just as the ceremony was about to begin Edward was offered a sip of brandy, but he brushed it aside and Mr Beresford cleared his throat.

"Dearly beloved, we are gathered together here in the sight of God, to join together this man and this woman in holy matrimony. . . ."

From outside there came shouts and a sound of hoof-beats, and Fanny remembered that a vast, weary army was tending its wounds all around them. Combat, however, was now at an end, and failing a visit from the Commander-in-Chief no-one was likely to get past the trooper on guard. Edward was very flushed and to Fanny's alarm he repeatedly closed his eyes. But the Chaplain carried on.

"Wilt thou have this woman to thy wedded wife, to live together after God's ordinance in the holy estate of matrimony? Wilt thou love her, comfort her, honour and keep her in sickness and in health, and forsaking all other keep thee only unto her, so long as ye both shall live?"

Edward's eyes opened, and he fastened them on Fanny.

"I will," he said clearly.

The more protracted vows caused him a certain amount of difficulty, but in the end he got through without error. Fanny was not sure that she was going to manage so well, but when the time came a kind of calm descended upon her and she listened with surprise to her own voice.

"I, Frances Catherine, take thee, Edward Charles Gordon George, to my wedded husband, to have and to hold from this day forward, for better for worse, for richer for poorer, in sickness and in health, to love, cherish and to obey, till death us do part, according to God's holy ordinance. And thereto I give thee my troth."

At the appropriate moment Sam Bright supported Edward's hand and placed the ring between his fingers, and somehow it slipped into place.

"With this ring I thee wed, with my body I thee worship, and with all my worldly goods I thee endow. In the name of the Father, and of the Son, and of the Holy Ghost. Amen."

It had clearly taken quite an effort for Edward to recite the last few words, but with some prompting he managed it. Wishing for a variety of reasons to keep the ceremony as brief as possible, the Chaplain offered one short prayer. Then he united their hands and made his closing pronouncements.

"Those whom God hath joined together, let no man put asunder. . . . I pronounce that they be man and wife together. . . ."

Edward had closed his eyes again, and for a few moments it was strikingly quiet. Then from the Brussels road there came the sound of a drum beat, and one or two ragged voices singing.

"Hey, Johnny Cope, are ye waking yet. . . ."

Mr Beresford turned towards Fanny, and held out his hand. "My dear Lady Ordley, let me be the first to congratulate you." He looked into her face. "This has been a difficult day, but I am sure you will never regret the ceremony we have just gone through. God works, you know, in mysterious ways, and there is always hope while life continues.

"Thank you, sir," she murmured.

"This was the happiest duty I have been called upon to perform in many days." He glanced at Lord Ordley, saw that he appeared to be asleep, and said quickly: "I'll leave you now, for I'm greatly needed, I fear."

Faraday was the next to offer felicitations, and on impulse Fanny kissed his grimy cheek. She thanked him again for the loan of his grandmother's ring, and said it would be returned to him as soon as a replacement could be obtained.

"I know how you must value it. It will be very safe, I promise you."

Faraday, who had flushed when she kissed him, seemed almost lost for words.

"I'll value it all the more, ma'am – your ladyship. It's been the greatest honour. Now, if Colonel Ordley don't need me any more I have a duty to report elsewhere."

A voice spoke behind them.

"You have a duty to sleep, Faraday. Ten hours, at the least. . . . Say I ordered it."

Faraday hesitated, then drew himself to attention. "Yes, sir. Thank you, sir."

After he had gone, the Marquis settled once more into silence. Looking hard at Fanny, Sam Bright said that he would try to arrange a corner of the barn so that she might rest and have a little privacy.

"You're very tired, my lady."

She smiled faintly. "So are you, I imagine. I haven't been in a battle."

"While the battle's on it keeps you going, ma'am." Ruefully, he examined the tattered remains of Lord Ordley's boots. "All over now, though. Boney's finished. There won't be much fighting for a while, I reckon."

"Thank Heavens."

She sank down on to the straw, beside the man she must now think of as her husband. Apart from the flush which still remained on his cheekbones he seemed markedly paler than before, and a cold terror gripped her. He was sleeping though, and after about an hour Captain Sulimann returned. He too offered warm congratulations, but she could tell that he was concerned about the condition of his patient, who no longer seemed to know exactly where he was. The Captain believed Lord Ordley was suffering a considerable degree of pain, and for this reason he administered several grains of morphia, as well as some other medicament.

When he had disappeared again, Fanny subsided on to the folded blanket which Sam Bright had now placed for her. She could hear him talking in a low voice to the trooper outside the door, and she could also hear the noises beyond, the horses neighing, the cries of wounded men, the rumble of wheels.

She did not feel as if she had just been married, she could not look ahead to any future. The world had drawn in around her, and now it was limited by the stone walls of a Belgian barn. Once or twice she thought about Lady Mapelforth and hoped she was safely on the way to England, but it was almost impossible to remember what her own life had been, just a few short hours earlier.

There was no longer any kind of flush in Edward's cheeks, and he lay deep in what she supposed must be a sleep induced by morphia. His breathing was fainter than it had been, and her only consolation was that it seemed fairly regular.

Hours went by, then she was startled by the familiar sound of a cock crowing. It was four o'clock in the morning, and Sam

Bright appeared beside her. Somehow he had obtained some coffee and had managed to brew it over a fire that had been lit outside. Sam wasn't fond of coffee. The Colonel, he said, hadn't much time for it either, but there was nothing else to be had, and it had been a long night.

The coffee was very bitter, but it revived her. While she drank Bright stood looking down at the prostrate body of his Colonel, then he bent lower and as he straightened again she saw something like a shake of the head. Fear gripped her.

"What is it?" she asked.

Bright rubbed a hand across his eyes.

"I'd say fever's gone, ma'am. He's sleeping deep and quiet."

Fanny bit her lip. No words would come, and after some hesitation Bright placed a hand beneath her elbow and drew her to her feet.

"Best to go outside, my lady. Take a walk. You'll be safe enough with Wilson on the watch and all's well here, just for now."

Outside in the cool of dawn, she stumbled and rubbed her eyes. A moon that was very nearly full hung among the branches of a stunted tree and one or two stars glimmered through mist, but morning was in the sky and low on the horizon small clouds drifted like scraps of cotton.

'Just for now. . . .'

The words clung around her, but she shook them off and fixed her mind firmly on the progress that had been made, the rush of thankfulness she had felt a few minutes before.

Wilson was leaning against the wall of the barn, his musket beside him. She wished him good morning and he saluted. There wasn't enough light for her to see anything else, apart from a few scattered trees and the solid outlines of farm buildings, but there was a smell, an unpleasant stench that had already begun seeping inside the barn.

Then she realised it was possible to see other things through the gossamer haze of dawn, and to hear things. Vague shapes were moving all around her, ghostly shapes that seemed to be busying themselves with some unseen operation. The chink of spades and thud of mattocks, the muffled sound of men's voices beat a message into her brain, and for the first time she understood what was going on under cover of the pearly light.

No more than a day earlier, she would have been petrified with horror. Now she just felt a leaden sadness for the loss of so many lives, the quenching of so much hope. The monster of Paris might have been demolished, but at what sort of cost?

She felt the dampness of morning on her cheeks. Not far away a thrush had started singing, feebly but with growing exuberance. Whatever might be about to happen now, another day was beginning.

Some time later a young Army surgeon arrived. Sent by Captain Sulimann, who had been obliged to rest for an hour, he took Lord Ordley's pulse, checked his bandages and placing a hand on his forehead pronounced the Colonel to be doing well. The fever was practically gone, and he was sleeping soundly – as the last dose of morphia had been administered some hours earlier, this might mean that the pain of his wounds had reduced. Provided there were no reverses during the next twenty-four hours or so, they might expect his lordship to make a good recovery. When he woke he should be offered repeated sips of water, and also a little warm broth, so soon as such a thing could be obtained.

"As for that commodity there," indicating the half empty brandy bottle, "I daresay he has received more than enough already. It is beginning to be understood that strong liquor is not always the best medicine for a wounded man."

Trying hard to forget the reference to reverses, Fanny decided to consult him about an issue that had been on her mind for hours.

"Should he not be moved to Brussels? Or at least to some place where he might be more comfortable? This is scarcely – "

"The road to Brussels is impassable, or very nearly so. Any such journey would take a number of hours, and would greatly increase the chance of re-opening Lord Ordley's wounds. He would suffer the most severe pain, and by the end of it might be very ill. If he is to be moved at all, I'd suggest you find some decent lodging near this place." He gathered up his bag, and bowed. "I wish you good day, madam."

Though Fanny felt as if she might never want to eat again, some sort of provisions had to be obtained. Sam Bright needed to eat, as did the troopers on watch outside – while one slept, the other remained on guard - and as soon as he was able to face it Edward Ordley must be persuaded to take a little soup, or something of that nature.

After a short discussion the batman set out on a foraging expedition, and when he came back it was to say that he had found a small company of Infantry eating mutton by the roadside. The mutton, no doubt, had come from a nearby field, the cooking they had done themselves. In consideration of the story he told them, they had eventually been willing to let him take a little away – in fact, he had secured more than enough for all of them to make a reasonable dinner - and in addition had given him some of the broth prepared for their own wounded. After that, he had gone to the nearby farmer's house, and there a good woman had let him take away two loaves, a pitcher of water and a carafe of wine.

Fanny was delighted his expedition had been so successful, but she herself could not face more than a piece of bread and a small cup of wine, and Edward was not yet awake. She watched as Bright and the trooper demolished sizeable helpings of mutton, then finally she gave way to Bright's urgings and went to rest on the pallet he had obtained for her. Lying on the Marquis's cloak, which had been spread over a layer of straw, she fell asleep at once.

XVI

When Fanny woke several hours later the barn was filled with bars of yellow sunlight. Several seconds passed before she could remember exactly where she was, then she leapt to her feet. Pausing only to smooth her gown and push the hair back from her face, she emerged from her corner to find Lord Ordley wide awake. The glitter had gone from his eyes, and at sight of her his bandaged head turned.

"Edward!" She dropped to her knees beside him. "You are better."

"You slept for a very long time." His tone was querulous. "Bright told me you were not to be disturbed, but I had begun to suspect you were run away with some French fugitive. You look - " Something of the old glow flickered in his eyes. "You look too beautiful to be safe. But then, you always do."

Only then did she become aware of the fact that her dress was crumpled, her hair cascading about her shoulders. Putting both hands to her head she tried to smooth the tumbled curls, but it was useless without a comb.

Edward lay watching her. "I wouldn't bother, if I were you."

She smiled at him. "Have you been awake for long?"

"Half an hour, perhaps. Bright fed me a quantity of disgusting gruel, then went off to make some arrangement or other. He had been hovering with cans of hot water. I think they were for you." With an obvious effort, he lifted his left hand and reached for hers. "You look as if you have been badly frightened. Is it because of me?"

"I have been anxious. But you are so much better – better than I expected to find you."

"I know. You looked just now as if you were expecting to find me very dead. But that would have been ill-mannered when I had just acquired a new wife." His fingers tugged at hers, attempting to draw her closer. "Fanny. . . ." He spoke huskily. "Are you going to kiss me?"

Leaning forward she attempted to kiss him on the cheek, but he turned his head so that their lips met. For a moment she allowed her mouth to rest against his, then she drew away.

He released her hand. "I want to get away from here." He sounded weary and petulant. "Sulimann was here a while ago, and he said 'not yet'. Does he imagine I'll fall apart if I'm separated from this heap of horse blankets?"

"Is there anything you need?" she asked soothingly. "Shall I go and look for Sam Bright?"

"No." He gritted his teeth, and she thought he tried to move. The pallor in his cheeks deepened, and as his body subsided into stillness all her fears returned.

"You must rest," she told him.

"I don't want to rest. They won't tell me anything. Sulimann wouldn't give me the truth. They say our victory is secure. . . . I know that. But I – I want to know who has died."

She felt tears rising, but checked them firmly.

"I think there is so much confusion. There may be many men who appear to be missing, but in fact are only wounded. Like you, Edward."

"Thousands are dead. I saw. . . I saw the Scots Greys, poor devils, and the Guards who held that cursed château."

"It was a very great battle."

Shortly afterwards he dropped back into sleep, and she felt relieved. He was not yet strong enough to deal with too much reality.

When Sam Bright came back she asked him if Captain Sulimann had said anything in particular, and he told her the Captain had been greatly pleased with his lordship, who was doing better than anyone could have expected. And Sam had other interesting news to impart. Having gone to seek out the farmer's dwelling-house he had found it quite a decent kind of place. The farmer had seemed friendly too, and his wife, and they had willingly provided more soup for Lord Ordley. Bread and a little meat, as well, and some apples, as he would show her ladyship. All would be paid for, of course, but still it had been a generous way to behave. Having gone through the Peninsular campaign Sam had seen a good deal of folk whose lives had been disturbed by war, and he had never found them so pleasant. He had even ventured to bring up the matter of his lordship not being strong enough to move just yet, and they had shown him a room – it was clean enough and quite large, and would be better than the barn. Maybe they could move the next day, if Captain Sulimann agreed.

In brilliant sunshine, Fanny walked to the farmhouse. There was still an unpleasant smell in the air and everywhere there was movement, but none of it mattered as it had done. She had come through moments of pure terror, and they had gone past. She was saddened by the tragedy that surrounded her – she would never forget it – but just at the moment she could not help being aware of the fact that it was not her tragedy. She had been spared. Edward had been spared, and she was deeply thankful.

No hens or cockerels roamed around the farmhouse – any that had been left to wander would probably have been seized by now, if not by the Allied Armies then by the French – but the kitchen door stood open, and when Fanny appeared the farmer's wife, Madame Counot, came forward to greet her. She seemed to be about forty years old, but she could have been younger. Weariness and anxiety were etched on her face, but she also had a quick, warm smile. In French, which Fanny understood perfectly, she said that her husband had thought they should leave, when the armies came so close, but it had not been as bad as they had thought it might be. The British troops had done them no deliberate hurt and they would not have suffered very greatly if it had not been for the loss of their crops, which had burned when fire spread from the château at Hougoumont. It had been hard, she said, losing the corn, but it was *le prix de victoire*, and others had paid a great deal more. During the last few hours, two of their farm boys had been helping the English soldiers to dig graves for their dead. She crossed herself as she mentioned this, and began muttering a Hail Mary beneath her breath.

Fanny felt immense admiration for her. Victory, after all, was not likely to place many rewards in the way of these uncomplaining Belgian peasants.

Proceeding to the discussion of practical matters, Madame Counot said she understood that miladi's husband could not be moved away until he was stronger, and if miladi thought it would be good enough he was very welcome to stay in their house. Perhaps miladi would like to come and see.

Beneath its smoke blackened rafters the kitchen was startlingly primitive. As Fanny stepped over the threshold several hens fluttered past squawking, and there was a small pig snuffling among the embers on the hearth. A selection of cats dozed nearby and a large dog growled from underneath the table, but sides of bacon hung from the ceiling, and bundles of sweet-smelling herbs.

As for the room being offered for Lord Ordley's use, it was large and clean and not at all uncomfortable. In normal times, Fanny was told, it was used as a family parlour, but already the parlour furnishings had been taken out and in their place a large bed had been installed. The bed's heavy frame could easily have been more than a century old, but the sheets and covers were spotlessly clean. Fanny guessed that it was probably the family's only bed, and her first instinct was to say they could not accept, but she soon realised her scruples might be misunderstood. The woman might easily take offence. Anyway, Edward needed a real bed, and the family would be rewarded.

It was only after leaving the farmhouse that she realised there had been no separate arrangement made for herself.

Obviously, it was assumed that she would share her husband's bed.

That night they remained where they were, but a supper of eggs and ham was sent over from the farm, with soup and bread for the wounded milord. Edward eyed the soup with disfavour, but nevertheless he consumed it, also managing a piece of bread. By the following morning he was strong enough to support himself on one elbow, and a surgeon sent over by Captain Sulimann declared him fit enough to be moved, at least as far as the farmhouse.

Slowly and carefully, Bright and Wilson edged his lordship on to a makeshift stretcher, then with the help of farm boys they carried him to his new accommodation. Deeply anxious, Fanny could only walk behind and be thankful for the surgeon's continuing presence, then wait while Bright got the Colonel settled in his bed. If she had been a real wife she would have been hovering round, supporting her husband's head and arranging his pillows, but she was not a real wife.

Not yet.

Summoning all her determination, she had spoken to the farmer's wife about separate sleeping arrangements for herself. As his lordship was in quite a lot of pain – she explained – it would not be comfortable for him to share a bed just at the moment. According her pallet had been moved back from the barn, and – very much better still – she later found that Bright had arranged for it to be placed behind a tall, screening cupboard. She was not at all sure what she would have done without the steadfast assistance of Bright. Placing the farmer's coarse sheets on her own bed, she gave Edward the fine linen ones she had brought with her from Brussels

Once settled in his new quarters, Lord Ordley slept for several hours. He seemed comfortable but deadly tired, and when he finally woke it was past seven o'clock. Madame Counot had prepared a dish of chicken and mushrooms – Fanny was afraid the chicken's neck had been wrung shortly after their arrival – and clearly he found this more palatable than the soup.

To accompany it he was allowed a glass of wine, and when the meal was over he lay still again, saying little.

At sunset Fanny took a short walk in the open air, and just as she returned a messenger on his way to Charleroi delivered a letter from the Duke of Wellington's Brussels headquarters. It came from an officer on the Duke's staff, and after glancing at it Edward passed it over to Fanny.

Standing by the window, she broke the seal and began to read aloud.

'*My dear Ordley,*

I was glad to hear that you had come through, in spite of the battering you took. I should not have been surprised to hear something worse, for I saw the Hussars go forward. It is being reckoned that during the two actions we may have lost close on seventeen thousand men, with perhaps twice as many being killed on the French side, and also the Prussians suffered greatly. Picton is dead, and Sir Alexander Gordon and William Ponsonby, and God knows how many others well known to us both. The job had to be done, however. Napoleon is gone back to Paris, where he may hope to make peace, but we shall never accept a Treaty while he remains and the word is they will quickly be rid of him.

I may not be in Brussels much longer, for the Duke will soon be gone towards Paris and I may travel with him, but no doubt I shall see you in London. When the years have gone by, I daresay you and I will both be glad to think we fought on the field by Waterloo.

It was signed 'Charles Woodford', and below the signature an additional note had been scrawled.

'*They say you are suddenly got married, and if so I wish you happiness*'.

Edward was silent for such a long time that she began to think he had fallen asleep. Then he said:

"My horse, Fedor. I think he was killed, but I cannot be sure."

Fanny sank on to the stool beside him.

"He cannot have suffered long."

"He was with me at Corunna, and at Vitoria. If that footpad

had not broken out of jail, he'd have been in his stable to-night."

Fanny's mind went back to a sultry afternoon in Brussels, and a tall dark horse that stood motionless under the trees. Edward had turned his head away, and she saw that it was to hide the weak tears that welled in his eyes. Her fingers tightened around his, and for a long time there was silence.

XVII

The farmer's wife, Madame Counot, quickly got used to preparing palatable meals for her English visitors. Bright and the two troopers still slept in the barn, but she fed them too, while her taciturn but good humoured husband kept them supplied with beer. Observing that Bright was often in attendance on Lord Ordley, she developed what she thought was a better understanding of Fanny's need for privacy, and the tall cupboard was supplemented by a precariously arranged calico curtain. A ewer and basin were provided, and these were followed by a comb – evidence that she had observed the tangles in miladi's hair.

The comb was delivered by Madame Counot's niece, a young girl called Gabriele. Gabriele's father owned a clothier's shop in Charleroi, but as the French Army advanced she had been sent away in order to avoid a possible sacking of the town. She had not been frightened, she said, when the battle commenced because she had trusted in *le bon Dieu*, as Monsieur le Curè had said she should, and *enfin*, all had been well, though she was very sorry for *les pauvres soldats*, and prayed for them every day. Enraptured by the sight of miladi's beautiful hair, she asked if she might wield the comb herself, and Fanny was surprised by her skill.

The following day Bright was despatched on a mission to Brussels. He was to visit Army Headquarters, at the same time bringing back clothes for his lordship, but he was also directed by Lord Ordley to call in the rue d'Orsay and collect her ladyship's band-boxes. Provided, of course, they had not been stolen. Nine hours later Bright returned, driving a wagon and bringing with him a variety of letters, and from the wagon he proudly lifted every single item of baggage abandoned by Fanny – among them, Pug's elaborately cushioned basket.

Helping Fanny to search through the few belongings that had not been carried away with Lady Mapelforth, Gabriele asked if she might take one or two items away to be smoothed by a flat iron, and when she had disappeared Fanny's eyes fell once again on Pug's satin lined basket. Dear Lady Mapelforth. . . dear Pug. She would keep the basket, she thought, until it could be returned to its owner.

She had begun to spend some of her time sitting in the kitchen, watching Madame Counot as she prepared pâtés and soups and cordial. Fanny felt quite comfortable with the hens – even, after a time, with the pig – and now that Edward was out of danger there was no need for him to be watched all the time. More to the point, she felt he had no wish to be watched all the time.

That evening, as they finished supper, she gathered up the plates and debris and prepared to remove them, but just as she reached the door he spoke.

"Fanny!"

She stopped, looking at him anxiously.

"Come back quickly, will you? You may find it diverting to spend hours discussing the finer points of farming in the Low Countries, but it's deucedly boring in here."

"I. . . ."

"Well, don't stop now. Take that stuff away, then come back."

When she returned, he indicated that she should sit down beside him.

"On our wedding night," he said sombrely, "you slept apart from me, wrapped in my cloak when you should have been in my arms. I am beginning to wonder if you would like to continue in the same style."

She was shocked, not just by the words but by something in his voice, something cold and questioning.

"You were hurt, Edward."

"Yes. I know." He reached out and took possession of her left hand, on which Cornet Faraday's ring shone dully. "I could not even give you a wedding ring, could I? It had to be borrowed."

"That scarcely mattered. You placed it on my finger."

"I should not have forced you to marry me that night – a wounded man, on the edge of a battlefield. If I hadn't thought I was going to die. . . . But I wanted to leave you safe. The Marchioness of Ordley, rich and secure."

During the last day or so she had emerged from profound darkness on to what had begun to seem like a sunny plateau. Now a small shadow touched her.

"I wish," she said, "you were not so rich. People will say that I married you because of that."

"Very possibly," he agreed. "People are liable to say anything. But when we married, my love, I was not thinking of your good name. I am a selfish individual, and I could not endure the thought of leaving you still in the clutches of that harridan Lady Mapelforth. When I think about her, insisting that you journey into France just at a time when Europe was once again about to blow up like a powder keg – "

"But nobody knew anything was about to happen," she pointed out. "You said yourself that France might be safe by spring. She had been ill and needed a change of air, a change of scene. And she was always very kind to me. In fact, I must write to her."

Without any warning a tear began coursing down her cheek, and he made a small sound that could have signified repentance.

"Sweetheart, don't! Of course you must write to her."

She wiped her eyes. "And we must write to your family. They may not know what to think."

"You may write to my brother Freddie, if you wish, or to your engaging stepdaughter – no, she is not your stepdaughter any longer, though she is your sister-in-law." He smiled wryly. "On the whole I think Freddie will understand very well what is going on. My other brother, Hugh, is with his regiment in India, and my sister has her own excellent sources of information. Let us think about ourselves. . . I want you to think about me."

Her eyes widened. "I do think about you."

"Yes. But I am not a patient man, and you are my wife." He watched her broodingly. "Why do you let that girl put your hair up? She has it dressed for dinner at Carlton House." Drawing her closer to him, he thrust his fingers in among the glossy coils arranged by Gabriele. One or two pins dropped on to the sheet that covered him, and as several more followed the heavy hair began to tumble round Fanny's shoulders. For a moment she tried to resist, to avoid being pulled nearer still, but when his mouth covered hers it took possession of her will. Fire seeped into her veins. . .

Abruptly she pulled away from him. Standing up, she pushed her hair back with fingers that were not quite steady

"You should rest, Edward."

He looked pale, but his face was still brooding.

"Should I? Very well. Go away, then. At this hour, you should be gossiping with Madame Counot."

That evening she took out her writing-case and penned a letter to Lady Mapelforth. It was not an easy letter to write. If she were to tell the complete truth about everything that had happened, her erstwhile employer might well suppose recent events had disturbed the balance of her mind, but on the other hand she needed to make it clear that she was now Lord Ordley's wife. In the end she managed to break the news in a manner that seemed not too startling, voiced the hope that they would meet again soon, and concluded with an expression of warm gratitude for all Lady Mapelforth's kindness. She asked to be remembered to Florence and Robert, and remarked that she missed Pug a great deal.

She ended up not writing to Justine.

The next day a surgeon arrived to change Lord Ordley's

dressings. Despite the obvious disapproval of Sam Bright he cheerfully accepted Fanny's offer of assistance – nothing could be more comfortable for the patient – and although there were difficult moments she somehow managed to get through without flinching, even when forced to look directly at the sabre cut that had almost severed her husband's arm. Afterwards Edward sank into a deep sleep, but when he woke some hours later his voice sounded stronger than it had done. Seated nearby, stitching a torn glove, Fanny felt his eyes upon her, and she looked up.

"Is there anything you would like?" she asked, moving quickly to adjust his pillows. "Shall I call for Bright - "

He shook his head slightly.

"I have everything I need."

"I believe," she told him, "you will be eating duck for supper. Cooked in wine. And there are strawberries. . . when the soldiers came Gabriele picked them and hid them away, and they are not rotted."

He lay watching her, as she studied the repairs to her glove.

"Tell me one thing, Fanny."

"Yes?" She had been about to inspect the other glove, but let it drop into her lap.

"Did you love your former husband, when you married him? He must have loved you."

"It was not that sort of marriage," she told him without hesitation. "Giles had loved his first wife, very much, but he needed someone to take care of his daughter and manage his house. Someone other than a governess. I was alone – my mother and father were dead, and I had no brothers or sisters. He became dear to me, but – but no more."

"Then you have never been *married*. . . ? You understand what I mean."

"No."

"That is what I believed." He sighed, looking upwards at the ceiling. "Throw those gloves away, Fanny. When we are back in Brussels you will buy new ones."

It had not taken her long to realise that Edward Ordley was

accustomed to getting his own way, and she began to wonder whether anyone – with the possible exception of his batman, his valet and those above him in the Service – had ever ventured to defy him over any matter whatsoever, even when it might have been very much to his advantage if they had done so. It seemed that he had adored his mother, and she in turn had idolised him. He also possessed a favourite sister, and it appeared likely that she had contributed to the spoiling process.

Hard experiences in the Army had undoubtedly saved his character, but they had not broken his slightly petulant will. Fanny's perpetual elusiveness made him irritable, and his resentment did not soften – rather the opposite – when very occasionally she allowed her head to rest against his sound shoulder.

After a few days he was allowed to get up and move about a little. His arm was mending well, and the fever had abated. He had several other wounds, among them a deep cut to the side of his head and a severed leg muscle, but none were causing any additional problems and every day he succeeded in recovering more strength. By the time another week had passed he walked outside, leaning on a stick, to stare at the parched edges of a battlefield. Anxiously Fanny walked beside him, but he did not speak and she had no wish to invade his thoughts.

Then on the tenth day of July two Cavalry officers arrived. As they entered Fanny melted away, but before their departure an hour later she was summoned back, and when she came into the room they leapt to attention.

"Lady Ordley!" The older of the two stared at her with undisguised admiration. "This is a very great honour! All the world is speaking about you, ma'am."

The younger officer smiled a little more quizzically.

"Crossing a battlefield in order to be married! Your ladyship is a heroine indeed."

Somehow Fanny managed to avoid offering any direct answer, but before they left she thought to ask them a question.

"I wonder, do you know – have you heard anything about Captain Maitland of the 13th Dragoons?"

The older officer looked at her sharply. "Why do you ask? Are you a relation of his?"

"I am acquainted with the lady who is to become his wife. Their engagement has not yet been made public."

"At present, Captain Maitland is considered to be missing. He may, of course, be lying wounded somewhere, but that is now regarded as improbable." He glanced away from her. "I am very sorry for the lady."

Soon afterwards they left, and when he looked at her face Edward's lips twisted ruefully.

"You cannot weep for them all, Fanny."

Later she learned that the two officers had brought some significant information. Having fallen back on Paris, Napoleon Buonaparte had apparently entertained hopes of remaining in power. However, aware that the Allies would never discuss peace with their Emperor the Assembly had turned against him, and as a result he had left the city and travelled to the port of Rochefort, where he had surrendered himself to the captain of a British warship. Now it was a question of deciding what to do with him. Meanwhile the fractured Allied Armies had marched into Paris, and King Louis was re-established at his palace of the Tuileries.

And in a day or so's time, Fanny was told, they would be travelling back to Brussels.

XVIII

Happening to turn up the following day, Captain Sulimann agreed that Lord Ordley was now sufficiently fit to undertake a carriage journey. He had been out in the wilderness for long enough, and from Lady Ordley's point of view their situation must often have been unendurable. It was a very happy outcome. At the start, he had not been at all sure the Marquis would come through so well.

"But you have had an excellent nurse," with a warm smile in Fanny's direction. "Without her ladyship, we might have been in greater difficulty. As it is, sir, you must exercise some care for a week or two longer."

Most of the wounded, he said, were now being accommodated in Brussels, though some - particularly those of lower rank – were lying in other towns, while many were still being tended out in the countryside.

One of the visiting Cavalry officers had promised to arrange a carriage, and early that evening it arrived. With a shock of real sadness Fanny realised that within hours they would be gone, and she knew that for all sorts of reasons she had not looked forward to this day. The last few weeks had marked a very special phase in her life, a phase that would never come back, and she wished their termination could have been postponed just a little longer. She was not looking forward to the moment when she would have to face the world.

Her first days at the farm had been marred by suspense and terrible anxiety, but then all of that had lifted. She and Edward had been together, yet without any of the problems that would come when their marriage became a reality. He had been getting better by the day, and yet still they had been hidden away from the world.

Sadly, she said silent good byes to the animals and the great peaceful kitchen, to the barn and the room in which Edward had begun recovering his strength. With real emotion she parted from Captain Sulimann and his assistants, from the padre – who had visited them from time to time, and who had altered the course of her life – and from Madame Counot. Wandering at the edge of the battlefield she thought of all those beneath the ground who would never return to their various homelands, whose relatives would receive no comfort, and at dusk on the eve of their departure that was where her husband found her.

Tears were pouring down her cheeks, and he put his good arm around her.

"Fanny, I know I've been a wretch to you lately, but you must always remember that I adore you. I owe my life to you."

She buried her face in his neck. "No, you owe your life to Bright and Captain Sulimann."

He kissed the top of her shining head, and her wet cheeks.

"You've had a lot to bear, sweetheart. But very soon now we shall be back in England, and then everything will change. We'll go to London and then to Ordley, my house in Hampshire. Whitcombe isn't of any great significance."

She clung to him, and gradually she stopped crying. She just wished she could let him know how much she dreaded the kind of change he was thinking about

Before they left, though, there was one spark of consolation.

After much apparent discussion within the family, Madame had told her that Gabriele would be willing to go with miladi as her *bonne* – even back to England. The girl's parents would be more than happy, for they had no doubt that she would be safe in the household of Monsieur le Marquis. And for Gabriele it would be a dream come true.

Without hesitation, Fanny said that she would be delighted.

Even though she had had no training at all, Gabriele was already an excellent maid, and she was also a sensible girl whose head would not be turned too much by the journey to another country. Whenever she wished she might go home – arrangements would be made for her – or her family might come to visit her. In the meantime, Fanny gave a solemn assurance that she would be well looked after

Though there was still some debris scattered round, the Brussels road was now clear. Looters had gathered up items of dress and equipment, decency and common sense had taken away the bodies. But still there were things to be seen. . . a leather pouch, a shattered boot, the torn and blood-stained jacket of a British infantryman. Fanny saw Edward's face as they passed these things, and she wished the coachman would go faster. She only wanted the journey to be over, and Edward to be safe in Brussels.

By the time they reached their destination he looked white and tired, but his voice was strong and he required no help as he descended from the carriage. They had been offered the use of two houses, one of them a tall building overlooking the park, the other, slightly smaller, positioned near the end of the rue d'Orsay. As it seemed likely to be less bother – as he observed – Edward had chosen the latter, but he had not asked Fanny what she thought, and she realised he did not yet think of himself as possessing a wife. Not that this troubled her in the least. Just for the moment, she had too many other things on her mind.

There were servants in the house, and two adjoining bedchambers had been made ready - as Lord and Lady Ordley were persons of quality it had been assumed they would require separate rooms. Fanny had anticipated this arrangement, but Edward, she realised, did not look upon it with favour, and she felt vaguely disturbed. One day soon they would become man and wife in every sense, but not just yet.

Their supper was served in a small dining parlour. The meal was excellent and the room very pleasant, but Fanny felt strangely at odds with her surroundings. She missed the simple comfort of the farmhouse, even the cooking of Madame Counot, and when a servant suddenly asked if her ladyship required anything further she looked around, half expecting to see Lady Mapelforth. At nine o'clock Edward retired to bed and as she knew Bright would be on hand she slipped away to her own room, where Gabriele, having finished unpacking, was waiting to brush her hair. More than ever, she was glad that she had Gabriele.

In the morning a bundle of mail was delivered. Most of it had been sent originally to the Duke's Headquarters, and as a few members of Staff were still in Brussels had been held until the Marquis of Ordley was available to receive it. Two of the letters were for Fanny, and looking at them eagerly she realised that one had been addressed in the familiar scrawl adopted by her former employer.

> '. . . *To the Most Noble the Marchioness of Ordley,*
> *By Care of His Grace the Duke of Wellington.* . . .'

Fanny knew very well how much satisfaction it would have given Lady Mapelforth to pen such a direction, but this in no way interfered with the pleasure she felt at receiving the letter.

Her ladyship described herself as being utterly and completely happy for Fanny. She owned that she was surprised, but only because young men in the Marquis's position were so rarely able to marry where they chose. She had, certainly, noticed a partiality – that afternoon in the park would always be vivid in her memory. In fact, it was quite amusing to recall that she had been a little anxious, at the time. Fanny had seemed so much like her own daughter, and in such delicate situations one could never be quite sure, not at any rate, with a man like Lord Ordley.

In the end, however, all had come right, and she asked for her very good wishes to be conveyed to his lordship. She said that she had suffered great anxiety when Fanny failed to join her in Antwerp, but that Sir John Coote had been the greatest possible support, reminding her how many friends they had in Brussels and how unlikely it was that any lady in Fanny's position would come to harm.

As for the great battle, just thinking about it still distressed her so much that she had quite given up reading the newspapers. Those dreadful lists seemed to go on and on, till in the end one almost forgot what a remarkable victory had been won. Among her closest friends there were several who had suffered the loss of sons or husbands, and truly it must never happen again. So many courageous and hopeful young men. She had really come to believe that war should be done away with altogether.

She ended by expressing the hope that Lord Ordley would very soon be restored to health and strength, and that before too long they would all be together in England.

Perhaps not surprisingly, Justine had written in a different style. As soon as she heard the news, she said, she had been in a dash to write and congratulate her stepmamma. She described Fanny's marriage as a 'happy event', and spoke very much as if all the circumstances had been entirely normal and the ceremony had followed tidily upon suitable announcements in the *Gazette* and the *Times*. No doubt, she supposed, they would think of visiting Whitcombe before long, and Fanny must know that she would be only too happy to direct preparations there.

She said nothing of her brother-in-law's recent brush with death, nor for that matter did she mention the conflict that had been dominating everyone's thoughts. Fanny accepted this as fairly normal conduct so far as her stepdaughter was concerned, but she was a little surprised that Freddie had not sent some more thoughtful message. Perhaps, though, he had written separately to his brother. If he had, it was quite probable that Edward would not show her the letter. Just as she would not be showing him the message she had received from Lady Mapelforth.

They stayed in Brussels just long enough for Edward to visit wounded friends and lodged a detailed report with representatives of his regiment. Still he had not seen the casualty lists as they appeared in the *Times* and the *Morning Post*, but these were not easily available, especially when Bright made certain they were not. He had received letters from his family, and over supper on their third evening in Brussels he brought up the subject of his brother Hugh, who had been serving abroad at the time of Freddie's wedding.

"Hugh is home from India at last, so you will be meeting him." He poured a little more wine into Fanny's glass, and re-filled his own.

"Is he in the least like you?" Fanny enquired. "Freddie isn't."

Edward hesitated, considering the matter.

"It's still difficult to be sure about Freddie, but Hugh is not like me. Much nicer, I'd say."

"I don't believe it," she responded.

He smiled. "You really are adorable, my love. One day I'm afraid you may suffer severe disillusionment."

"I never shall, Edward. Not about you."

"Well, soon we shall be back in England, and everything may begin to look rather different. I think we should delay going to Ordley for a week or two, for I shall probably need to be in London. Of course, a lot of people will have gone to the country, or to Paris. Apparently our occupying Army is being followed by a large section of society."

"You would have been in Paris," she reminded him, "if you had not been hurt."

"Yes, well, I'm happy to have escaped that duty. We shall be perfectly civil to the French and most of them, no doubt, will be civil to us, but they've suffered a great defeat, poor devils, and I shouldn't enjoy that. None of our fellows will. I believe we'll stay only long enough to ensure Louis's government is in place, and there is order." He studied her over the top of his glass. "Anyway, there'll be quite enough of our acquaintance still in London, and you are going to be the toast of society. I shall show you to everybody, and they'll adore you."

She looked thoughtful. "People will stare at me and ask questions about me, and about you. How did you become entangled with me, what a pity someone didn't rescue you in time. The Marquis of Ordley married to a complete outsider – that is not going to please everybody."

"It doesn't have to please everybody. Only me. I agree that by the time we arrive in England richly embroidered stories of our 'death-bed' wedding will almost certainly be circulating throughout London. . . the beautiful new Lady Ordley, who was so entirely heedless of her own safety that she risked canon-fire to reach my side. You couldn't do better than that if we'd been married in St Paul's. There may be malice in some of it, but most reasonable people will think it a trifle far fetched to suppose you undertook an uncomfortable journey across a rather nasty battlefield simply for the purpose of improving your financial condition – even, for the sake of acquiring a title."

She sighed, a long and rather ragged sigh. "Lady Mapelforth took most of my clothes home to England. Until I get them back again, I shall look like Cinderella."

"Then you must do some shopping in Brussels. There are bound to be one or two dressmakers working, and you will barely have to lift a finger before they come running. I'll give you a draft on my bank account – I had meant to do that, anyway. Of course, when we're back in England proper arrangements will be made. And, Fanny – " before she could start to argue about this – "my sister Georgiana will be meeting us at Dover. I have written to say more or less when we may be expected, and she will stay in the town until we arrive. I am sure you will get on with her. She's a fairly easy person to know, and she'll help you. She dresses very well herself, and when we reach London she will put you in touch with the right people."

"That will be nice," Fanny heard herself say mechanically.

Across the table, she glanced at her husband. That morning he had been visited by another senior Army surgeon, and had been told that his wounds were still healing well. The bandage had gone from his beautifully brushed dark hair, and nothing more than a light dressing covered the gash that had made it necessary. His right arm was supported by a sling, which meant that one sleeve of his crisp, previously unworn uniform jacket hung empty beside him, but he looked strikingly handsome and a lingering pallor merely served to emphasise the blackness of his almost feminine eyelashes. Shaved to perfection by Bright, and a little grim about the lips, he looked devastating, and she could imagine the effect he would have back home in England.

With painful clarity she recollected that afternoon in the park – the afternoon of the seventh of June – when everything had swum in a haze of heat, and the Marquis of Ordley had sat astride his black horse in the shade of a protecting tree. Six weeks had gone by since then, and people no longer swept through the park in carriages, or walked beneath the trees for their amusement. The Richmonds' ball was something many people would like to forget, and Brussels itself was given up to the victims of war. The tall black horse was dead, and its rider fortunate to be alive.

And she herself was no longer Fanny Templeton, companion to Lady Mapelforth. She was the Marchioness of Ordley, about to be launched on English society and full of vague fears because it all seemed quite unreal, and anyway she was by no means certain that she would be able to acquit herself favourably. Even in the bosom of her husband's family.

As Edward had predicted, she had no difficulty in acquiring a few essential additions to her wardrobe. Lady Mapelforth had patronised several modistes and milliners and most of these were still working, or attempting to do so. Even if this had not been the case, Lord Ordley's name – as Fanny soon discovered – would have opened almost any door. And since expense seemed hardly to count – although she was somewhat slow to take advantage of this – she left Brussels very suitably if unostentatiously equipped to face the demands of her new life.

A friend who was still awaiting news of a brother had offered them the loan of his yacht, and just over a week after entering Brussels they set out on the road for Antwerp. While Sam Bright rode alongside, Gabriele and the baggage followed in a second vehicle, and for most of the way Fanny was alone with her husband. But he was very silent, and she realised that he was brooding still – if perhaps for the last time - over all those who would never be going home.

After a lengthy carriage drive, and one night spent in a large and rather uncomfortable inn, they found themselves setting sail for England.

XIX

There was not much wind, and it was noon on the following day before they came in sight of Dover. Not – as Fanny suspected – wishing to appear feeble when they came to step ashore, Edward had spent much of the time resting, but when the pale cliffs of Kent finally slipped into view he appeared beside her at the yacht's starboard rail.

"Well, we're nearly there." A slight smile played around his lips. "As you may have noticed, it was quite choppy at one moment. I wondered if you might not find such conditions uncomfortable, but Bright tells me they scarcely troubled you."

"They scarcely troubled Gabriele, either, and that was truly a relief," she told him wryly. "As for me, I had no right to be troubled. My father was a sailor, an officer in the Navy. He. . . ." She hesitated. "He died at sea. At the battle of Trafalgar."

"Trafalgar!"

"We used to live in Sussex, near the coast, and when my father was at home I sometimes went out in a small boat. I was never afraid of the sea. Then after Papa was killed we moved away into Kent. My mother worried a great deal about my education and always watched over my lessons, but she died only six months after Papa. I was eighteen."

"And it was then that you started to earn your own living?"

She smiled. "Yes. I became governess to Justine. If I hadn't done so, I might not have met you, my lord."

Their hands were linked, and he carried hers up to his lips.

"It's an odd thing, Fanny, but I know so little about you.

You're such of a wisp of a creature, and people have not listened to you enough. I have not. In future, I shall make sure no-one neglects to pay you proper attention."

"You have paid me attention," she pointed out. "You married me, Edward."

He kissed her hand again.

"The wisest thing I ever did."

The white cliffs came closer, and soon they could pick out the little town of Dover, huddled behind a flotilla of ships. The yacht dropped anchor, and they saw the harbour. Various figures were moving on the quayside and two in particular – a man and a woman – appeared to be staring fixedly at their own vessel. The woman was making excited gestures, and something like a bright green feather waved beside her bonnet. The man, who was a good deal taller, wore a scarlet coat.

"It's Georgie," Edward said with a pleased smile. "She can't keep still for a minute. And that's my brother Hugh. . . I think he has a glass trained upon us."

Momentarily panic-stricken, Fanny glanced down at her own dress. It was jaconet muslin, and the colour was sky blue. Worn with matching gloves and soft kid slippers it had seemed exactly right, but now she was uncertain. Edward's sister frightened her.

"I-I must go below. . ." she began.

"So that that you can fuss about how you look?" He seized her hand and held it tightly. "You look enchanting, and Georgie will love you. As for Hugh, you'll be likely to break his heart. It cracks rather easily, I believe."

Going ashore was uncomfortable for Edward, as coming on board had been, but as he stepped on to the quayside his sister hurled herself upon him. She clung to him, sobbing, for nearly a minute and when she looked up her face was drenched with tears.

"Edward. . . *Edward*. . . ! We – I believed we had lost you!"

Her arms were round his neck, all but strangling him, and his new scarlet shako tilted sideways. If it hadn't been for the vigilance of Bright, who had stationed himself nearby, the Marquis might have been precipitated into the murky waters behind them.

A faint breeze stirred Fanny's jaconet muslin, and she realised Edward's brother was eyeing her admiringly.

"Well, as you see, I'm not lost," Lord Ordley pointed out soothingly.

Georgiana's outfit was the clear green of a water melon, and she was so beautiful that Fanny could hardly believe her eyes. Such a complexion must be rare indeed, especially when it went with huge dark eyes and silkily sweeping lashes. She had the Marquis's night dark hair, only in her case it had been twisted into glossy ringlets; and she had his swift, warm smile, and beautifully even teeth.

"But if you only knew what a nightmare it has been! Roly Rutherford is dead, and Charles Carmichael. George Danvers lost a leg, and Colonel Archdale – "

"Here, hold on, Georgie!" Apart from the fact that his curly hair was a warm brown, Lord Hugh March looked very much like his brother. "Edward seems a bit rocky to me, and if you don't take care you'll have him in the sea. Besides, it's more than time I was presented to my new sister."

The Marquis put a hand behind him, and drew Fanny forward.

"Here she is," he said. "Fanny, allow me to present my sister Georgiana, who is Duchess of Knaresborough, and my brother, Hugh March. Georgie, you're going to make an awful mess of your face."

But miraculously her tears had dried. Looking at Fanny, she let out a shriek of delight.

"Oh, how delightfully, *ravishingly* pretty! My dear, you're going to be such an advantage to our family. But I simply cannot imagine you being married on a battlefield. I cannot see you on a battlefield. You don't look in the least like it, somehow. All that smoke, and gunfire. . . you must be quite extraordinarily brave!"

"I have no doubt she's very brave indeed." Hugh smiled at Fanny. "My dear Lady Ordley, I'm delighted to welcome you, and if Edward does not object I should like to salute you in an appropriate manner – "

"Please do."

His brother's voice was a trifle dry, but Hugh waited for no further encouragement. Bending forward he kissed Fanny on both cheeks, then lifted her gloved hand to his lips.

"And now," said the Marquis, "if everyone has finished saluting each other in an appropriate manner, perhaps we may leave this draughty jetty and make for the inn over there."

He looked as if he needed to sit down, preferably in some place where no-one would mention battlefields for at least half an hour, and Fanny was concerned by his sudden pallor. As a little group of curious onlookers parted to let them through, she slipped her hand inside his arm and drew him along the quay. At the bottom of a short, rough incline her place was taken by Hugh and Sam Bright, and she fell behind, but at the inn door he looked round for her, and she knew that his tired smile was meant to give her reassurance.

She and Georgiana had been walking side by side, and the young Duchess had barely ceased to chatter about the horrors her new sister-in-law must have endured. But so far she had not welcomed Fanny with any real warmth, or even attempted to touch her hand. Edward Ordley had known his sister since she first appeared in her cradle, and that might have been one reason why his brow was so noticeably creased by the time they lowered him into a chair in the coffee-room.

XX

Georgiana and her brother Hugh had not travelled from London quite by themselves. In addition to their own servants, they had brought one of the most eminent surgeons in London. Mr Gisborne had once been attached to the Navy, and consequently he was very familiar with the kind of injuries likely to be inflicted during conflict. Once Edward had retired to his room and rested for a while the surgeon waited upon him, and half an hour later Fanny was given his verdict.

Lord Ordley, the surgeon said, was making an extraordinarily good recovery, but some of his injuries had been of a serious nature. His right arm might never regain its former strength, and his right leg – in which muscles and tendons had been damaged – might also have suffered incurable damage. To speak plainly, he could be left with a limp. Mr Gisborne had advised his lordship that he might very well need to consider resigning his commission.

When she had heard everything the surgeon had to say, Fanny hurried upstairs to see her husband. He had been given one of the largest rooms the inn had to offer, and the summer evening light did not reach very far beyond its wide, single window. He was seated beside the window, looking out on a crowded yard, and she was frightened by something she saw in him, something limp and inert.

"Edward. . . ?" She put a hand over his. "Mr Gisborne seems pleased. You are doing so well."

"Am I?" He looked up at her. "My right arm will not be the

139

same again, and I shall walk with a limp. Because I am going to be completely useless, I had better not delay about resigning my commission."

"But you were not going to stay in the Army, you told me so. You have so many other things to think about, and. . . the war is over, Edward."

"The war is over. Yes, that appears to be true." Lightly toying with her fingers, he stared down into the yard.

"You're tired. Perhaps we should not think about dining downstairs."

"I shall not, but you must do so." He smiled slightly. "Fanny, you are like a candle in a dark corner. You clear away the shadows. Or at least, you make them seem not so important."

She tried to insist that she would take dinner upstairs with him, but he told her it was not to be considered.

"I mean to do as I am ordered, and recover my strength. I have seen enough of my family for one day, but you should become better acquainted with them. If Georgie becomes a little overpowering, you will no doubt get support from Hugh – just so long as you keep him in his place."

"Afterwards, I'll come and see you," she promised. "Only you may be asleep."

"I may be. And your room, I understand, is several miles away."

"The inn is packed, and your brother had great difficulty in securing rooms."

"M'mm. No doubt. Well, you might as well be far away, since you refuse to share my bed." He smiled up at her, ruefully. "Of course, you could give me a kiss."

She let him pull her towards him, just for a moment. When she drew away he was looking mildly gratified, and her cheeks were flushed.

"Now, go and sample the local cuisine. Don't let Georgiana gobble you up with the gooseberry tart. And don't. . . don't come to look at me, later on. You might lose your way in these ancient passages and end up in the landlord's own chamber. . .

or – which might be slightly worse – in Hugh's."

As she left him, he was still looking thoughtful.

When she entered the family's private dining-parlour, an hour later, she was dressed in all the beauty of ivory satin, and there was a fillet of pale green velvet in her hair. They were all waiting for her – the distinguished doctor, her brother-in-law and her sister-in-law. The young Duchess was looking displeased because apart from anything else she had been kept waiting for a full ten minutes, and the one thing she abhorred – as she often told her friends – was being kept waiting. Nevertheless, she smiled at Fanny quite brilliantly. She was, she confessed, still very concerned about her brother Edward, and felt quite strongly that she should see him again before he settled for the night. Perhaps after dinner she might spend a little time with him.

But Mr Gisborne said emphatically that he must advise her Grace against such an idea. The Marquis needed to recoup his strength, and for one evening at least would be very much better left to himself. With a not very good grace Georgiana accepted that a medical man's opinion must, in such a case, be respected, then she turned her attention to the dish of local carp that had just made its appearance. She had never, she declared, been so hungry in her life, nor had she ever felt so drained of strength - but it had, of course, been a desperately emotional day. She rather quickly drank two glasses of champagne, then returned to the subject of Brussels and the quite horrifying 'goings on' over there. She commanded Fanny to give her a complete picture of everything that had happened, and in particular wanted to know all about the now infamous ball. How could the Duchess of Richmond have been so ill advised as to allow such a nonsense to *proceed*. . . ? It was something Georgiana would never understand. Her own husband, the Duke of Knaresborough, had been far too occupied to allow of their going to Brussels, but in any case she had felt not the slightest wish to go. And to be dancing, with Napoleon on the march towards them – hundreds of those young men were now dead. She had never heard of anything more shocking. She began recalling names, officers of her acquaintance who had apparently been lost, and asking whether Fanny could recollect seeing them at the ball, until Hugh intervened abruptly.

"Really, Georgie, that is more than enough! Fanny has been obliged to think about such things every day, quite apart from what she has suffered on Edward's account. I daresay she won't wish to talk about any of it, not yet at any rate, and I shouldn't blame her."

Since Fanny entered the room he had hardly been able to take his eyes off her, but there was sympathy as well as admiration in his eyes, and she felt grateful to him.

As the meal went on Georgiana did not talk any less, and possibly inspired by champagne she moved rather swiftly to the subject of Fanny's marriage. One could only abhor the kind of gossip that would be certain to spread, but just to begin with she owned that she had thought – she had *wondered*. . . . A widow, marrying a man who was in such danger, and the whole thing so sudden! She had been quite firm with anyone who had spoken to her, for she knew her brother too well to suppose him capable of stupidity. But he had been badly wounded, and must have been a little out of his mind. Thoughts were bound to arise, and one could not honestly wonder at it.

What Fanny began to realise what was being suggested, she felt a little sick. She had always known there would be some kind of talk – she had even discussed the matter with Edward – but she had not expected her husband's sister to speak in such a way. At any rate, not to her face.

Apparently heedless of the surgeon's presence, Georgiana began asking questions about the ceremony that had united her brother with Fanny. Under cover of professing horror at such a nightmarish ordeal - and investing Fanny with all the attributes of a selfless angel and an intrepid Edith – she succeeded in informing herself on one or two important points. The marriage had, of course, been conducted by a clergyman. And there had been witnesses? How absolutely charming. . . a young cavalry officer and Edward's own batman But, well, but what about the license? Surely, where there had been no time for banns, one could not be married without a license?

Fanny said nothing.

"Well, I know what I think!" Avoiding Hugh's eye, her Grace looked amiably around the table. "I think we should have another ceremony, performed here in England, with all the family present and every obligation observed. *That* would delight everyone!"

"Rubbish!" Hugh said shortly. So shortly that his sister stared at him in surprise.

"Of course I am not really suggesting," she went on, "that there was anything amiss with the way this marriage was conducted, only that many people may imagine there was. I mean. . . . in such a situation, I daresay, one is quite exempt from the need to trouble about such things as licenses. Only the world won't think about that, and I am concerned for Fanny. The poor girl needs advice and support, and I imagine she has had little enough of either. She has been obliged to care for Edward, and nurse him, and indeed I can quite believe he may not have survived if she had not married him. Very likely, she gave him the will to live!"

"Almost certainly," the surgeon from London agreed. He had been feeling increasingly irritated by the implications behind her Grace's remarks, and only wished there could have been some other woman present to defend Fanny, who in his opinion was entirely suited to be the Marquis's wife – indeed, to be the wife of just about anyone, however exalted, who was lucky enough to get her.

And there was no doubt about it, Hugh was in complete agreement with him.

"I'll tell you what," the Marquis's younger brother observed, lifting his glass to Fanny, an example emulated by the beaming surgeon, "if I was ever to find myself dying on a battlefield – though since I'm leaving the Army pretty soon there may not be much danger of it – and someone like Fanny was there, braving all the smoke and shells and mangled horses and what not, just to get to my side, I believe I'd die happy, just hearing her say 'I will'. Mind you," he added obscurely, "if that didn't bring me back from the grave, nothing would."

Fanny felt herself blushing, but she had to make one thing clear.

"It wasn't quite like that. The battle was almost over before I left Brussels, and by the time I got to Edward there was very little gunfire."

"But you must have seen such things," Georgiana put in sympathetically.

"Yes. There were dreadful things."

"I'm very sure there were," the surgeon agreed with feeling, while an inn servant re-filled his glass. "From all the accounts one hears, it appears to have been a particularly violent business. And having seen for myself the destruction wrought upon Lord Ordley, I can only deplore the barbarity of modern weaponry and wish there might be some other means of settling disputes between nations."

"Not sure I can agree with you about that," Hugh murmured, staring thoughtfully at the veal pie that had just been set down in front of him. "There's a lot of us would have very little to do if it wasn't for the odd war, now and again. I'll admit that this business with Boney had been going on far too long, but I regret that I was not in at the death. It would have been something, to have fought at Waterloo. For the rest of our lives, Edward will have that on me."

Georgiana shuddered dramatically.

"Well, I am very thankful you were merely on your way home from India. To have been in danger of losing two brothers on the same day. . . . At least Freddie can't fight any more, thank Heaven."

As she spoke she half glanced at her new sister-in-law, and Fanny realised she was thinking of Justine. Until that moment she had almost wondered if Georgiana knew of the connection between them. Now she understood. She could see exactly what

Freddie's sister had thought of his marriage – and why, in Fanny's hearing at least, he had never made any mention of her existence.

"Anyway, Hugh," Georgiana continued, "if some girl had been persuaded to marry you, as you lay wounded, it might hardly have caused any talk at all, for *she* would not have been in any danger of becoming a very rich widow. The poor thing would have been left with nothing but a large number of debts and a run down manor house in Gloucestershire."

There was silence. Georgiana glanced at Fanny, then went on hurriedly to introduce entirely fresh topics of conversation. An uncle who was spending too much at the gaming tables, the servant problems besetting a pair of elderly aunts, a favourite cousin's distress over her husband's supposed involvement with an actress. Even the problems caused by her own two boys.

"Richard does not like his tutor, and for a child of eight he has the most frightening command of language." With the tip of a fork, she tapped something that lay on her plate. "This is very fine veal pie. If you want to find the best sort of cooking, go to a respectable inn. That was what Mamma used to say."

By this time both men had fallen silent, and Fanny had no desire to speak. They heard a coach rumble into the yard, and the shouts of an ostler. In the street, two passers by seemed to be starting a fight. And Georgiana thought of something else.

"You know, Hugh, I had poor Jane with me yesterday, almost the whole of the morning. You recall how she wept over the lists from Waterloo. She is better, of course, but still quite low in spirits. I nearly brought her with me today, I thought it might divert her. But then I supposed it might not be wise."

"Good God, I should think not."

Georgiana shrugged. "I only said I thought about it. Naturally I realise she couldn't have borne it, under the circumstances."

Fanny felt tired and confused. She had no idea what they were talking about, and she wanted to get away – away from Georgiana.

Soon afterwards the Duchess rose to her feet. Covering a

yawn, she declared that she really could not go on struggling to eat, and if she attempted to stay awake any longer she would be quite unfit to travel the following day. Fanny stood up at the same time, but though they left the room together her Grace's vocal powers seemed temporarily to have been exhausted. Breathing a hasty good night, she left Fanny standing alone in the passageway.

It was no more than nine o'clock, but the summer night had closed down and stopping beside a window she saw that stars were glittering above the long line of a coach house roof. Laughter drifted up from the coffee room, and voices. Comprehensible voices. She was back in England and it should be a happy time, but just at that moment she felt a wild, irrepressible longing for the barn where she had been married, and a farmhouse kitchen in which pigs snuffled beneath a table.

Carefully and quietly, she opened the door of her husband's room. He was sound asleep, with a single candle burning beside him and one hand flung out carelessly across the sheet. Creeping closer she bent to kiss the hand, so softly that her lips barely touched. She wanted to slip in beside him, to lie there motionless until dawn. But she could not do such a thing and anyway Gabriele would be sitting up, waiting for her.

That night she lay awake for a long time, listening to the muffled noises of Dover. Then the inn's sheltering arms closed round her, and she fell into a deep sleep.

XXI

Declaring that she needed to be back in town, Georgiana left the following morning. While Fanny took breakfast alone she contrived to spend a few minutes with her brother, then watched by the landlord himself she climbed into her carriage. Hugh protested strongly, saying that it was too early – they hadn't even seen Fanny, yet – but in the end he capitulated and climbed in after her.

Glimpsing the vehicle's yellow wheels as they rolled out of the inn yard, Fanny felt a sense of relief. But she knew the reprieve could not last for long.

The surgeon had suggested that Lord Ordley should take a further day's rest before going on to London, and – partly, Fanny suspected, because it would give time for his own carriage to arrive – Edward agreed. He was not so happy about the idea that Mr Gisborne should remain and travel with them, but Fanny pointed out that the surgeon had been brought down by Georgiana, and they could hardly refuse to convey him back again.

While Edward sat in his room writing innumerable letters Fanny and Gabriele went for a walk around the town, then in the evening Mr Gisborne joined Lord and Lady Ordley for a quiet supper. Once, during the day, Edward had mentioned Georgiana, describing how happy and engaging she had been as a girl, before she was married. It was obvious that he knew how she felt about Fanny – since their private chat it would have been odd if he had suspected nothing – but very clearly he was anxious to defend, even justify his sister's behaviour. Fanny came close to expressing her own views on the subject, but just in time she checked herself. She understood that her husband felt deep affection for Georgiana, and she also knew it would have been miraculous indeed if none of his relations had objected to his choice of bride.

In time, perhaps, everything would be different. In the meanwhile she would grit her teeth and put up with Georgiana.

Edward's travelling chariot, when it arrived, proved almost as comfortable as it was magnificent to look at. Its four gleaming bays drew them at astonishing speed out of Dover and on to the London road, and every time they stopped its brightly emblazoned door panels brought inn servants scurrying to be of use.

The roads were thick with dust, and more dust lay across the fields and the sprawling woods, but tears stung Fanny's eyes more than once, not because of the dust but because the woods and the ripening corn and the small, contented villages were so beautiful. There was one corner of Belgium that she would never forget. But nothing could compare with the splendour of Kent, seen on a warm morning of late summer.

The rest in Dover seemed to have restored much of Edward's strength, and by the time they neared London he had also recovered his spirits. As they rattled over the cobbles Fanny felt increasingly uneasy but the Marquis of Ordley was approaching his London home, and when they finally entered St James's Square he did not even seem dismayed to find several dozen of his household gathered outside to receive him.

His lordship's secretary and valet were standing at the top of the steps with an imposing butler and a handsomely clad housekeeper beside them, and on either side straggled a family group of maids and footmen, porters, cooks and grooms. The steps were put up and as her husband was helped down on to the pavement Fanny heard a ragged cheer go up. The butler stepped forward, and she caught a few of his words.

"Your lordship. . . glorious victory. . . injuries. Gratitude to God. . ."

Edward smiled and shook his secretary's hand, then the butler's, and the housemaids curtsied like a ripple of small wavelets on a beach. When Fanny appeared the curtsies were repeated, but a little more stiffly and nervously, and as she climbed the steps it was the housekeeper, not the butler, who moved forward.

"I bid you welcome, my lady." Another stiff curtsy.

Fanny smiled at her. "It's Mrs Roper, isn't it?"

"Yes, ma'am."

"I hope we shall be great friends."

They entered the cool vestibule, and its echoing tranquillity calmed Fanny's nerves. She had known that the houses in St James's Square were among the finest in London, but she had never been inside one of them and for a moment she gazed in amazement at the soaring columns and the white staircase, the gleaming mosaic floor. It struck her that the floor was as slippery as the surface of a frozen lake and she glanced anxiously at Edward, but she had no need to worry. Bright and Mr Gisborne had now been joined by a third individual, and she realised that this was Caxton, the valet who looked after Edward whenever he was at home.

They really had come a long way from the farmhouse at Waterloo.

Mrs Roper explained that they had not been sure what to do, but in the absence of directions she and Mr Batsford – the butler - had decided it would be best to provide Lord and Lady Ordley with a suite of rooms on the ground floor. The small green parlour – which the former Marchioness had particularly liked – had been made into a bedroom for her ladyship, while a pleasant room not too far away had been got ready for the Master. There was a small closet, which would be convenient, and the yellow drawing-room was close by. As for his lordship's library, it was just a step or two away.

Their baggage was carried in, and within minutes Fanny

found herself in her new bedroom, where she was quickly joined by an excited Gabriele.

When she next saw her husband, he was reclining on a sofa beside the long windows of his own room. Green lawns and summer blooms could be seen outside the window, and she remembered that houses of this sort often had large secluded gardens. Edward had been provided with a stiff brandy, and he told her Mr Gisborne had just left.

"He assures me that I and my cuts and bruises have been quite unaffected by the journey from Dover. However, if I wish to go on progressing at this rate – as he expresses it – I must do as I am told and take appropriate rest. As you see, I should not dream of disobeying him. I mean to be fit again before the summer ends. My life at the moment is in a peculiar state of confusion, and I must sort it out."

"What do you mean?"

"I mean, leaving the Service will involve me in some re-arrangement."

"Yes, of course. I see."

He told her the surgeon had left as swiftly as possible, begging to be remembered to Fanny but declining all offers of hospitality. He lived, it seemed, in Baker Street, and his wife would be awaiting his return for dinner.

He held out a hand to her.

"Sweetheart, it's wonderful to be back. Back in England. . . back in St James's Square. I know the house must strike you as a bit of a mausoleum, but it's fortunate there is so much space, at least down here on the ground floor. Old Batsford and Mrs Roper were confronted by a bit of a problem, but I think they've worked things out rather well. I gather your rooms are not too far away?"

"No. No, they're not far away." She bent to inhale the scent from a bowl of roses that had been placed close to his elbow. "I'll leave you to rest, Edward."

"Very well."

She saw that his eyes were heavy with tiredness, and when

she had closed the window a little she tip-toed out of the room.

Later that evening, as she ate her supper in lonely state, she felt inclined to envy Mr Gisborne, and his comfortable existence in Baker Street.

XXII

The next day they said good bye to Sam Bright. Fanny was distressed, the more so because Bright was being sent back to barracks, and Edward showed signs of irritation.

"Caxton," he told her, "has been with me since my father first decided I should have a valet. He does an excellent job, and I could not allow anyone else to interfere with that. While I was on campaign Bright was second to none, but he would not understand the life that I lead at home. He is re-joining his regiment because that is what he wishes, but there is little chance he will see combat again. Before too long he will be out of the Service, and when that day arrives there will be a cottage awaiting him, either at Ordley or at Whitcombe, whichever he prefers. When he and his wife are established there, you will be able to call upon him and share reminiscences."

"I didn't understand," Fanny said.

He smiled at her ruefully. "You ought to trust me, Fanny."

At the end of July London would normally have been empty, but this was no ordinary year. Significant numbers having drifted across to Paris others had decided to stay in the English capital, and over the following week a steady trickle of visitors arrived in St James's Square. Many were friends of Edward Ordley and when these arrived they were shown directly to the library, where they remained until removed an hour later by Batsford. Others – exclusively female – had come to inspect the new Marchioness.

Most of them were already acquainted with Fanny, or at least they were acquainted with Mrs Templeton, who had usually been better known as Lady Mapelforth's companion. Mrs Templeton had been a pretty young woman, nicely bred and pleasing, and most had thought she might find herself a very decent sort of second husband. Someone with a respectable income, perhaps a baronet. She had not done that, though, she had secured the Marquis of Ordley.

Seated in the small yellow drawing-room – her own small yellow drawing-room, which in itself seemed very odd – she answered their questions as best she could, then after the fifth or sixth visitor knew she could stand no more for a while. In the hall she encountered Hugh, who was just about to leave after a conversation with his brother, but she hurried past him. Having told the servants she would see no-one further until the following day, she was crossing the small lobby when she became aware that Batsford had just opened the door to someone else. Someone whose voice was strikingly familiar.

"I am very certain Lady Ordley is at home, and I can assure you she will not refuse to see me!"

Hurrying back across the mosaic floor, Fanny told Batsford that it was all right.

"Lady Mapelforth. . . !" A lump rose in her throat. "I am so very happy to see you!"

XXIII

Before taking a seat, Lady Mapelforth paused to inspect her surroundings.

"You know," she confided, "I was never in this house before. My dear Fanny, those covers. . . ! And the curtains – that sort of velvet is always the most costly. But expense, I suppose, is barely a consideration." She sat down, and accepted a glass of ratafia. "My love, I cannot tell you how delighted I was to get your news. Surprised, of course, but that's all over and done with. When I first got back to England, I'll own, I was in the most wretched state. I hadn't the least idea what might have become of you, and after that terrible journey. . . ."

She enquired after the Marquis's health, remarked what a shocking thing it was that such a fine man should have been cut about by murderous Frenchmen, then launched into a detailed description of the trials that had befallen her. The road from Brussels, so jammed with carriages that they had barely been able to move, the flea-ridden inn at Antwerp where the landlord had refused to speak English and Sir John had been forced to remember what French he had managed to learn at the Paris Embassy. Worst of all, though, had been the horrible sea captain who had thought it a joke to suggest they might make more space by throwing Pug overboard.

It had been the most exciting thing she had ever experienced, and she would probably repeat the story until her dying day. Fanny was keenly interested, but also she was happy just to listen. Despite the alarming nature of Lady Mapelforth's recollections, she felt soothed by the sound of them. It was almost as if the last few weeks had never happened, or at least had not happened in her own life. Then with a jolt they both came back to the present.

"I must say, my dear. . . ." Lady Mapelforth stared at her. "You do appear quite pale. It's very understandable, of course, but I hope you are not allowing your spirits to become too much oppressed."

"No. No, of course not. Everything is all right now."

"Well, I'm pleased to hear it. You have been through a good deal, and to hear, as you must do, that there is so much unkind talk. . . ."

Fanny moistened her lips. "Do you - have you heard very much talk?"

Lady Mapelforth looked uncomfortable. "My dear, it really is not so very bad. Most people would not dream of breathing a word against you. But you know as well as I that there will always be some who are ready to take pleasure in scandal."

"Why should they find my marriage scandalous?"

"You mean you did not know?"

"I thought perhaps one or two people might think - "

"My love, I am very sorry to have been the means of telling you, but I thought you must have understood. Fanny, you went through shocking danger to be at Lord Ordley's side. You found him lying severely wounded, and very soon afterwards became his wife. If his lordship had been some young Captain of Dragoons with perhaps five hundred a year, nobody would have been shocked in the least. They would all have thought you a heroine, as indeed you are. But your bridegroom was the Marquis of Ordley, with I don't know how many estates and a position at Court. He was on the edge of death, as you say yourself, and you married him. You *must* see how it can be thought to look. No-one, of course, was surprised to learn that he had become fond of you – I saw it myself, and felt most anxious. But marriage!"

"So they are saying. . . ." Fanny's voice was stiff. "They are saying I persuaded my – I persuaded Lord Ordley to marry me?"

Lady Mapelforth looked flustered and repentant. "My love, I should not have said anything. It is unpleasant gossip, but I am sure not at all widespread. Forget what I said, you really must not regard it. Do not ever think, Fanny, that I don't set people right when I hear such things. You have suffered enough, my dear. To be so newly a wife, and not know whether you may soon be required to purchase your weeds!"

"Edward is recovering his strength," Fanny said with difficulty. "He will soon be quite fit again."

"Well, I am very glad to hear that. Upon my word I am, for your sake. Who has the care of him, now that he is back in London? It will be one of the best physicians, I suppose."

"Mr Gisborne is looking after him."

"Ah! Then I expect he is quite safe. They say that Mr Gisborne has been asked for at Windsor Castle."

"The Army surgeon was excellent," Fanny said, feeling an urge to speak up for Captain Sulimann. "He saved Edward's life."

"Did he, indeed?" Lady Mapelforth's face softened. "I see you have been in great anxiety, my love, and I am sure there is nothing worse, especially when you have been a widow once already, even though you barely look old enough to have escaped the schoolroom. However, I have just now made up my mind what I am going to do. I heard the other day about a litter of Pug pups – they are only a week or two old just at present, but when they are two or three months they will be able to leave their mother, and I mean to purchase one for you. They are the greatest solace in the world, and hardly any trouble at all."

"You are very kind." Tears sprang up behind Fanny's eyes. "How – how is Pug? Your Pug, I mean."

"He is extremely well, my dear, though I swear he misses you." Again, she looked round the pretty drawing room. "This is very charming, I must say. And you look perfectly suited to your new position. That gown could not be more becoming. Have you done a great deal of shopping since you arrived in London?"

Fanny decided not to remind her that the dress in question had been purchased in Brussels, some weeks earlier.

"Not a great deal."

"Well, no doubt you will soon begin. Perhaps we might visit a warehouse together, one day. I always valued your advice, Fanny." She leaned forward a little. "Now do tell me, who was that atrociously handsome young man who was leaving just as I came in? I noticed that he was in uniform. Is he just back from Brussels also?"

"That was Edward's brother, Lord Hugh March. He has recently returned from India, and I think means to leave the Army very soon."

"Well, I am glad to hear it. Three brothers in the Service, all in danger of being cut to ribbons! I know that many people were shocked when Lord Ordley remained in the Army after his father's death. A man with his responsibilities – it was very unusual and I think quite improper, though you may disagree with me. But I daresay all that will change now that he is married. Lord Freddie, of course, has already been obliged to come out." A thought occurred to her. "I only recollected the other day that Freddie, of course, is married to that minx Justine, who gave you so much trouble." She added: "I imagine I can guess what the Duchess of Knaresborough thinks about *that* connection." A clock on the mantelpiece began chiming noon, and she started up. "I quite forgot the time! I should have been home a quarter of an hour ago."

Before leaving she kissed Fanny affectionately, and patted her hand.

"My love, I truly wish you all the happiness in the world, for I'm sure you deserve it. I am afraid I shocked you just now, but there are some things it is best to be aware of. Nearly everybody, you know, thinks you nothing less than a heroine, but there are some – and though you may say I am wrong, I should be inclined to place the Duchess of Knaresborough among them – who will choose to call you an adventuress. So pray be on your guard." They moved towards the door, and then she stopped. "I have not told you, and the happiest news! You will recall Edwina Palfrey, who was in such despair over Captain Maitland? Well, they thought him lost, of course. But just the other day Edwina had a letter, and it turns out that he is safe. He has been taken care of at some place near the French frontier, and very soon will be well enough to come home."

With tremendous sincerity, Fanny said: "I am very happy for him. And for Edwina."

Lady Mapelforth nodded. "Well, good bye, my love. No doubt we shall meet again soon, and when we do I hope you will tell me Lord Ordley is quite himself again."

When she had gone, Fanny remained still for a long time. Then she hurried away to the seclusion of her own bedroom.

Later that afternoon she went to the library, where Edward was working at his desk. After his brother's departure he had spent some time talking to the agent who managed his Hampshire estates and to his secretary, Mr Rochdale, and Fanny was afraid he might have tired himself, but he seemed fresh and alert as he stood up to greet her. His uniform gone, he was wearing a dark blue coat and if anything it became him even better than the flamboyant array of Army dress. Pulling open a desk drawer, he took something out of it.

"Come here, Fanny!"

Cautiously she took a step towards him. "What is it?"

"Give me your hand – your left hand."

She obeyed, and almost before she knew what was happening Cornet Faraday's ring had been removed, placed on the desk and replaced by a golden band that looked a little heavy on Fanny's slender third finger. After this Edward opened a velvet lined case from which he extracted a glittering diamond. The diamond was slipped on to a different finger, and he studied the result with satisfaction.

"There! A little late in the day, perhaps. But the result, I think, is entirely satisfactory. What do you think?"

Fanny had been taken too much by surprise to say anything immediately. When she did express an opinion, it was obviously not quite what he had expected.

"It's a very handsome ring, Edward. They are both. . . beautiful rings. But ought it not to be blessed, or – or something? The wedding ring, I mean?"

He gazed at her in astonishment.

"Blessed? My darling girl. . . ! Any necessary blessing was got through when we were married. The padre knew that Faraday's ring was a temporary expedient which would be replaced as swiftly as possible. Now, I have effected that replacement. Perhaps not so soon as I might have done if our situation had been entirely normal, but that being said, the job is done and it is now time to send Faraday back his ring – with, of course, a note of appreciation. Which, if you like, may be signed by us both."

"Yes, of course. I should like to sign the note."

He put his head on one side. "I think you have become attached to Faraday's ring."

She wondered how he could fail to understand that everything connected with those moments in the barn would always be inexpressibly dear, to her at any rate. She had always known Cornet Faraday's ring would have to be returned, she had even looked forward to the moment when Edward would place his own ring on her finger, but she had not imagined anything like this.

"I suppose. . . I have just got used to wearing it."

He smiled. "Well, that's all right. Now you can start getting used to your new and entirely rightful hallmark of bondage." Without glancing at Faraday's ring, he dropped it into the open drawer. "Now, how do you like the diamond? Perhaps I should have asked whether you might prefer some other stone, but this has been in our family for more than a hundred years. It was worn by my mother, but for you I shall have the diamonds re-set. There are bracelets and a necklace to go with it. All should arrive here within the next few days – they are being cleaned and set and should be ready, I hope, in time for Georgiana's ball."

"Georgiana's ball?"

"Yes. She went to the country after leaving us in Dover, but could not endure the quiet. She says, because too much is going on. In a letter I received this morning, she writes that she is coming back to town and is giving a ball on the twenty-sixth day of this month. She believes it will bring people flocking back to London, and I'm sure she may well be right. Georgie usually gets what she wants. Any ball is a delicate matter just now, because of the way people feel about our losses, but she believes we should celebrate victory... after all, as she says, they are doing so in Paris."

"I see." At that moment, Fanny could not bring herself to add anything further.

"And that is all you have to say? About the jewel, I mean? If it doesn't please you we'll drop it back into the vault from which it was taken."

His tone was rather sharp, and Fanny started as if waking from a trance.

"It's magnificent," she said quickly. "But should it not belong to Georgiana?"

"No, it should not. As I told you, it was worn by my mother, and before that by my father's mother. You understand how such things are done. These are family jewels, and now they will be worn by you. There's a lot of other stuff besides, pushed away out of sight, but if you'd rather not have any of it – "

There was a hurt look about his mouth and eyes, and an increasing touch of resentment.

Remorsefully, Fanny said: "Of course I should love to see all the jewellery, but why should it be worn by me?"

He stared at her, one eyebrow raised. "Why should it not? One day it will belong to our son's wife and no doubt she will wear the lot, as women often do. Why do you believe you ought to be different?"

She felt mildly shaken. Could it really be that one day. . . . When she didn't answer he limped closer, and she realised that during these last few weeks she had forgotten how tall he was.

"Fanny, what is to be done with you?"

"What do you mean?" she asked, looking up at him.

Unexpectedly he put his arms around her, pulling her close.

"You are locked away somewhere, and I can't reach you. It is as if you don't want the world to suspect you are real – as if you don't want to *be* real. Sometimes, I think you don't want to be here."

"Edward!"

"You have done a wonderful job of looking after me, but you will not accept that I am almost fit again, so – " He stepped back, looking down at her. "Fanny, I will make an arrangement with you. When my sister's ball is over we will leave London and go down to Ordley, as we ought to have done already. We will take only the servants with us, and will receive no visitors for several weeks. Will you like that?"

"Yes. I should like that."

"Then it's settled." He turned back to his desk, but a thought occurred to him. "While we are on the subject of jewels and keepsakes, what has happened to the signet ring I left with you?"

"I carry it with me." She lifted the fine chain around her neck, and when the ring appeared she covered it with her fingers.

"Good Lord!" He appeared genuinely astonished. "Well, but you can't need it now. I'll have another made, small enough to fit your finger."

"I don't want another. And in case you should think I am going to return this one, let me tell you I shall not do so under any circumstances. You may do as you please with Cornet Faraday's ring, but you gave me this one and I mean to keep it."

He laughed, then he saw her face. "Sweetheart, I didn't mean to distress you. Keep the ring, if you wish to, but another might serve you better."

He had put an arm round her shoulders, but unexpectedly she wrenched herself away.

"I have told you, I don't want another signet ring." She knew she sounded childish and unreasonable, but she couldn't help it and for the first time since he had known her, her green eyes flickered with anger. "There are some things, Edward, that are more important than getting in touch with one's jeweller and having things altered or enlarged or made smaller, or – or turned into something else. There are some things that cannot be re-set, or re-polished, or put away in a vault. . . ."

Her lip quivered, and a large tear brimmed over. As it trickled down her cheek, he handed her a cambric handkerchief.

"I stand reproved, my lady," he said softly. "I don't mind telling you, I envy that ring. I beg you will remember, however, that it is no more than a ring."

That evening, Fanny received a note from Georgiana.

'My dearest sister,' she had written, *'I feel that I made you uncomfortable, the other night in Dover. I was so happy and relieved to see Edward that perhaps I was not quite ready to share him, and Hugh says you may have been offended. Or wounded, or some such thing. Anyway, if that is so I beg your pardon, and entreat that we may be friends in future. I long to see you at Knaresborough House on the twenty-sixth, and as I daresay you mean to buy a new gown, and I shall certainly do the same, can we go shopping together? If you agree, I shall call for you at eleven o'clock to-morrow morning.'*

Fanny read the letter several times, and decided that it was perfectly genuine. She had been inclined to dislike Georgiana very much indeed, but could see now that she had probably been too hasty. If she were truly as spiteful as she appeared to be, Edward would not be so fond of her. And though on the whole she would have preferred to go shopping alone, there could be no better way of getting to know her new sister.

XXIV

Punctually at eleven o'clock the following morning Fanny stepped into the cushioned interior of Georgiana's carriage and they set out upon their expedition. First they headed towards a silk merchant in Leicester Square, and while Georgiana darted about eagerly Fanny purchased several lengths of the finest cream-coloured gauze she had ever seen in her life, then they climbed back into the carriage and drove off towards Bruton Street, where they were to visit the premises of a certain celebrated modiste.

"Her prices," Georgiana said happily, "are beyond everything, but neither of us needs to trouble much about that. Anyway," with a conspiratorial smile, "you and I are both certain to look bewilderingly beautiful, so it would be very strange if our husbands begrudged the money."

Never having heard anything quite like this, Fanny found it difficult to reply. But Georgiana never seemed to require a response.

Having always recognised the fact that her hair colour presented certain difficulties, Fanny had come to understand what suited her and for the most part tended to favour subtle shades, in particular creams and mauves and very delicate greens. Her companion, however, had bolder ideas, and within minutes the Duchess was declaring that she would like above all things to see her new sister in flaming reds and tawny apricots. Alternatively, perhaps, in stark black and white.

"Your true character is not gentle and passive, Fanny, though some people may be deceived into thinking it so. If you had been such a very meek little kitten you could hardly have married Edward as you did."

The modiste, Madame Haubert, suggested that her ladyship should not dress in such a way as to cover up her youthful appearance, but Georgiana again disagreed.

"I feel," she said, "we should be thinking in quite a different way. Obviously you are still young, Fanny, but you have so much confidence and *élan*. In all the circumstances you could hardly be a frightened bride, and that is so important for Edward. You know," she went on in a lower tone, "I see you now as quite the perfect wife for my brother. He has left the Army, and that means he will soon be paying much greater attention to inherited responsibilities. He will entertain a great deal, both in London and in the country, and the last thing he will need is a timid, inexperienced bride. The ideal wife for Edward, I am now persuaded, could only be someone like you. A woman who will preside over his many homes and ensure his personal comfort, who will have the courage to be a good hostess and never find herself at a loss - as some empty headed young thing, however engagingly pretty, almost certainly would."

Rather startled, Fanny once again found it impossible to venture any reply. But as her sister-in-law talked very fast indeed, touching upon a wide variety of different subjects within a breathtakingly short space of time, she felt her own silence probably went unnoticed.

When it came to bonnets and shawls, slippers and half boots, gloves and silken hose, pelisses and petticoats, it was difficult to do anything but give the Duchess her head, but Fanny did succeed in resisting suggestions that she needed – immediately – to purchase a great number of dresses. If she had listened to the urgings of Georgiana, she would have left Madame Haubert's elegant premises with a greater number of day dresses, formal gowns, capes and redingotes than she would have been likely to wear before most of them went out of fashion. As it was, she merely purchased three morning gowns and an elegant velvet cloak. But then they came to the question of a gown for the Victory Ball, and here she quickly sensed there was likely to be conflict.

Georgiana, it emerged, had already selected the gown she planned to wear herself. Consequently she was free to fix her attention upon Fanny, and within minutes she had pounced upon something she declared to be perfect. Emerald green satin, overlaid by cobwebby black lace – it was, Georgiana said, one of the most striking gowns she had ever seen in her life, and nothing could possibly be more suitable for Fanny. It would do the most incredible things for her hair, and also it was so well fitted to her character.

Not only, Fanny realised, would the green dress make her look at least ten years older than she was, it would also cast her firmly in the rôle of a widowed temptress with a particular skill for ensnaring wealthy and impressionable noblemen. She had already settled, more or less, on a confection of ivory satin covered by pale golden gauze - a peach coloured rose nestled at the waist, and the neckline came just short of being too revealing. Out of consideration for Georgiana's feelings she agreed to try the emerald satin first, but then she turned back firmly to the golden gauze.

She was standing in Madame Haubert's main salon, studying her own reflection in a looking glass, when they were unexpectedly addressed by a masculine voice.

"Upon my word," Hugh March declared, "if you're planning to wear that for the ball, Fanny, you'll have'em falling flat at your feet."

"Hugh!" His sister threw him a glance that was distinctly irritable. "How on earth did you come in here?"

"I saw your carriage outside and guessed you had Fanny with you, so I thought I'd venture over the doorstep. I told them who I was, and they said I might come so far as this room, provided I was careful to behave properly."

"Well, you may go away again. No decision has yet been taken, but I have advised Fanny to pick that heavenly green satin over there. It will do far more for her than the gold, which is much too pallid – I personally would not consider it for a moment."

"But then, my dear sister, you are not Fanny," Lord Hugh remarked, going over to inspect the green satin at closer range. "That," he observed, "puts me in mind of Mamma's sister, the one we aren't supposed to talk about. Ran away to India with some other woman's husband."

"I wish you will not be so absurd," Georgiana snapped. "The dress is perfect, and I have told Fanny what I think. However, it is for her to decide and if she has already done so there is nothing more to be said. Now, *do* leave us alone," giving him a small push. "This is no place for your sex, and Fanny has to change again. You may wait for us in the carriage, and if you endeavour not to annoy me any further you may come back with me for luncheon."

But Hugh shook his head. "Not if it means calling in St James's. I was there this morning, and Edward threw me out. Came storming out of the library – limping, actually, but you don't regard that with Edward – and said that so far I was concerned his wife wasn't home. Wouldn't be, for a fortnight."

"Well, upon my word!" Georgiana threw a look at Fanny. "He really has been behaving very oddly. It will be pleasant when we find we have the old Edward back again."

"I'm so sorry, Hugh." Fanny felt she had to apologise for her husband's temper. "I am quite sure he did not think – did not mean you to take him seriously."

"Didn't he?" Hugh's handsome, amiable face was almost glowering, something which was remarkable in itself. "Well, I'm pretty certain he'd have run me through with a small sword, if he'd had one handy and I had not pretty smartly recollected an engagement."

"Well," Georgiana said briskly, "I suggest you both come back with me, and Fanny may go home afterwards."

Fanny would have liked to refuse, but in the circumstances it was scarcely possible. Her purchases were piled into the carriage

– with the exception of those, the golden gauze among them, that required minor alterations – and they were all whisked away to the Duchess's house in Grosvenor Square. During luncheon Georgiana chattered brightly and incessantly about her plans for the twenty-sixth, and the considerable number of people who had already promised to attend her Victory Ball, and Hugh was unusually silent. As soon as was decently possible, Fanny thanked her sister-in-law and escaped to St James's Square.

Edward Ordley was in his library again, and when Fanny entered she found that he was sulking noticeably. She had been absent for longer than he approved, and he did not hesitate to point this out. She realised that his injuries and lengthy convalescence had imposed considerable strain upon him, and noticing his drawn, slightly sulky expression felt guilty because she had left him alone so long. She would willingly have foregone the golden gown and all her other purchases, if by so doing she could have prevented that look. She did not say anything about Hugh, who had obviously been unfortunate enough to provoke an outburst of fleeting irritability, but she did ask why his secretary was not with him.

"I've given Rochdale leave to take himself off, down to the country. He'll join us later on, when we're at Ordley."

"But don't you need his help?"

"No, madam, I need a little pleasant society. This evening, I think I shall go to White's."

Fanny would have been perfectly happy to escape attendance at Georgiana's ball, but that was not a possibility and if it had been Gabriele at least would have been very much disappointed. Happily, Gabriele was settling in extremely well. Her English was improving by leaps and bounds, and though she undoubtedly relished the special respect accorded to her position, she got on well with the other staff. Even, it appeared, with Caxton, who was not always easy to deal with. As she helped her mistress to dress for the ball she became increasingly excited, and the final result caused her to gasp with delight.

"Madame, *vous êtes éclatante*! You look very beautiful."

"If I do, it is mainly due to your work and this dress." Fanny surveyed herself critically. "But there will be a great many elegant ladies at the ball, and I don't think I shall look very impressive beside them."

She was sincere in saying this, but she was nevertheless looking forward to the moment when she would show herself to Edward, who had not so far seen the golden gauze. Apart from anything else she wanted him to see that the dress had been worth what seemed to her a very shocking expenditure of his money.

When she appeared he was already in the lobby, pacing up and down beside his butler, who was waiting to open the door for them. Half unconsciously Fanny stood still for a moment, and as Edward stared at her his eyes became intent. He went on staring for several seconds, then he glanced at the ornate gilded clock that occupied a table by the library door.

"It's past nine o'clock," he remarked. "If we delay any longer, the crush on my sister's stairs will be unendurable."

The August night was warm, but Fanny felt an unexpected chill and was glad of the cape that a footman hastened to place around her shoulders. As she settled in the leather scented interior of the carriage she was acutely conscious of Edward's presence beside her, but he said nothing at all, even when they rolled into motion. He was wearing a blue velvet coat and white satin small clothes, with diamonds glimmering in his cravat and on the buttons of his waistcoat. He wore orders, she noticed, and for the first time saw that he had acquired a new signet ring. Despite his silence and the demon – whatever it was – that possessed him, she derived the keenest pleasure just from knowing that he was beside her.

They rattled at speed through dimly visible streets and squares, while the link boys' torches cast long shadows and every passing beam of light drew sparks from Fanny's golden dress. As they approached the carriage-lined fringes of Grosvenor

Square lamps shone through the night like golden eyes, and rolling to a halt before the entrance of Knaresborough House they found the tall building a blaze of light. *Flambeaux* lined the pavement, while rows of footmen in powder and gold lace guarded the steps against a horde of onlookers.

Inside the effect was even more splendid, with Corinthian and Ionic columns soaring amid the magnificence of crystal chandeliers. Grecian statuary guarded the entrance, and the crowded staircase was decorated with cascades of flowers and richly swagged draperies of velvet and damask. Over a babel of voices, music drifted down like an echo from the stars.

As they climbed through the crush Lord Ordley placed a protective arm about his wife, though they did not exchange so much as a word. At the top of the stairs, where guests were still being received, they were both embraced by Georgiana - whose high bosomed dress of pearl grey silk was sufficiently striking to set her apart - and for the first time Fanny met the Duke of Knaresborough. Plainly much older than his wife, he looked dignified in a black satin coat. Having kissed Fanny's hand he retained it very briefly in a gentle hold, and she thought his smile was kind and paternal as he said how delighted he was to meet her at last.

Fanny recognised some, but not many of the guests. An astonishing number of people seemed to have heeded Georgiana's call and returned from the country, and as they moved towards the ballroom Fanny cheered herself with the thought that in such a crush little attention was likely to be focused on any one individual - certainly not on herself. In a room adjoining the ballroom they encountered Hugh, and she was relieved to see Edward greet him with something approaching cordiality. Relief turned to dismay, however, when she realised her husband was about to abandon her. Above the din of voices and music she found it impossible to hear exactly what he said to her, and as he walked away through the crowd she turned in bewilderment to his brother.

"I thought. . . ."

"Edward's going to join the Duke and a few cronies. He's not quite up to dancing yet, you know." Hugh offered her his arm. "If you'll allow me to escort you, I'll be only too happy."

She placed her fingers on his arm but at the same time looked back, following the progress of Edward's dark head.

"Perhaps I should go with him."

"No, Fanny. When a man wants to talk about the war and that kind of thing, it's not the time for his wife to be there too. Besides, you're here to dance and give us all the pleasure of looking at you." His mouth twisted wryly. "I don't know whether I'm permitted to say so, but you're looking amazing."

She danced with Hugh, then with a cousin of his, then with a middle aged viscount who wanted to know if she had witnessed the charge of the Royal Scots Greys. After that a number of people were presented to her, their faces quickly melting into a blur. She knew quite well that some of the women arched their eyebrows as she passed, but she didn't allow that to bother her, nor did she pay much attention to admiring glances. That evening she had wanted her husband's admiration, and if she couldn't have that nothing else seemed to matter very much.

Rather daringly, she danced the waltz with a young officer from a foot regiment. As they whirled beneath the chandeliers he told her he would never forget the honour she was bestowing on him, then went on to ask if it were true that at the moment of their marriage Lord Ordley had been given 'not much above half an hour'. She could not remember, afterwards, what she had said in reply.

She danced a lot, mainly because dancing was preferable to conversation. Hugh re-appeared several times, bringing her iced lemon water – on such a hot night she refused to drink champagne – and once she sat on the stairs with him, watching a display of fireworks through the tall gallery window. At ten o'clock she let him take her in to supper, but it was very warm by this time and the sight of food left her with a feeling of nausea. Eyeing her with some anxiety, Hugh urged her to accept a glass of champagne.

"Take a few sips, at the least."

She tasted the drink, which made her feel dizzy. Edward wasn't in the supper room, or at any rate she could not see him.

"I'd like to go outside," she said desperately. "Is there a way. . . ?"

Hugh set his glass down. "We'll go downstairs and out through the small drawing-room."

It was cooler outside, but not so cool that Fanny felt the need of a wrap. Pursued by faint sounds from the supper room they walked up and down between pale statuary and carpet-like strips of lawn, finally seating themselves upon a wide stone seat. The voices behind them became more noticeable, and there were one or two shouts of what sounded like approval.

"They're toasting the Duke," Hugh observed, looking up at the few stars that were visible.

"Oh, Hugh! I should not have brought you out here."

He shook his head. "Heard him toasted a hundred times, just in the last month. You're not feeling too cool?"

"No, I'm much more comfortable."

There was the sound of a pianoforte, then a woman's voice. The music was soft and mournful, and it crept beneath Fanny's skin.

"Love and death, I suppose," Hugh said with an odd laugh. "Usual thing."

One or two other guests had now come out to stroll between the trees, but Fanny did not recognise any of them and it occurred to her that years might pass before she felt entirely happy in the world inhabited by her husband.

"Do you mean to leave the Army?" she asked Hugh.

He shrugged. "War with Boney's over, and I'm fed up with India. Took me half the voyage home to get over that last fever. Troubles in America may grumble on, but fighting over there's not to my taste, either. Too much like killing within one's own family, even though they won't be quiet and let our ships alone."

"What will you do?"

"Lord knows. Edward has talked of giving me a manor, but there wouldn't be much land. I shouldn't know how to run the place and there would never be money enough for an agent."

"You'll have to find a rich wife."

"That's what they all expect, but I don't much like the thought of being tied to a girl I don't care for, just so that she'll keep the duns away. Mind you, until – " He checked himself. "Anyway, who would look at me?"

She was about to assure him that many nice girls would look at him, then all at once she noticed something. Several couples had begun drifting back inside the house, but there was another bench on the opposite side of the garden and she saw that a tall man had just seated himself there, with a girl beside him. The girl had pale golden curls, and a nearby torch showed that she was dressed in ethereal blue, with silver slippers just peeping from beneath the hem of her gown. As for the man, he was... Edward.

She swallowed, and felt as if the evening chill deepened.

"Hugh, who is that person sitting over there. . . . with Edward?"

Hugh peered into the gloom. For a second or two he seemed tongue-tied, then he appeared not to see anything. Finally, he said:

"Oh, I see, yes. . . little Jane Armitage. Known her all my life, but this light's so damned confusing."

"Is she the same Jane your sister was so concerned about when we were in Dover? The one who had shed so many tears over the lists from Waterloo? The one who was so very nearly brought to Dover?

"Er. . . yes. That's the same Jane. Emotional little thing. Always had a great fancy for Edward, who was years older than her, of course – still is, for that matter." He laughed uncertainly, then coughed. "I think he's seen us. I think they've both seen us."

"But we have not seen them." She stood up. "You said there was a lily pond in this garden, and a very fine walk. I should like to see them, in the starlight. It's so peaceful out here."

She placed her hand on Hugh's arm, and obediently he led her away along a path lined by slender maple trees. Apart from misty starlight there was nothing to illuminate the walk, but eventually it opened into a place where more torches flickered and a small fountain played beside a lily pond.

Standing still, Fanny released Hugh's arm and turned to face him.

"Hugh, I want you to be honest with me. Does your sister have a great interest in seeing Edward married to that girl?"

"Good God, Fanny! He's married to you!"

"Never mind that. Miss Armitage is extremely pretty, and I daresay she's of very good family. Isn't she?"

"Lord, yes," he admitted. "The best. When the old Earl of Reith finally departs this life, Jane's brother stands to inherit. There's a huge amount of money in the family. They have estates near Ordley. Marching side by side, and all that."

"Which makes it perfectly understandable," Fanny observed reasonably, "that Georgiana should have become upset when she heard about me. I didn't understand at first. All those hints about the possibility that our marriage might not be legally valid. She is hoping, of course, that it may be annulled."

"*What?*" She saw the shock in his face. "Do you realise what you're saying?"

"Yes, of course."

"She knows Edward too well."

Fanny was silent.

"He's madly in love with you. Oh, yes, he is. He married you when he thought he might be dying, because he could not endure the thought of not doing so. He would like to tear out the throat of any man who can't help but cast an eye on you – it's the reason he turned on me, just the other day."

A waning moon had now climbed into view, flooding the walk behind them with silver light, but she stood looking down at the dimly visible water lilies.

"I think he didn't mean to marry," she said slowly, "until after he had left the Army. But as you say, he had known Jane Armitage all her life, and I think it very likely they had an understanding. She is extremely suitable, and he must have known it was what Georgiana wanted. He has such a great regard for your sister – "

"Not such a regard that he'd toss his life away to please her! He may have thought about Jane in the past, and Georgie may have talked about her, but he's always been careful not to get caught by the other sex, and I must tell you that he's had his pick. Women would follow him through the jaws of death. . . the title and the estates are only part of it, too. He's so damned handsome they can't drag their eyes away from him. I've always envied him that, I can tell you."

"I don't think you need to envy Edward," she said gently.

"Don't you?" He looked rueful. "You're being kind, though. You're the sweetest and dearest woman I ever met." He caught her hand and lifted it to his lips. "If only I could have got in first, before all that drama at Waterloo. I even had to miss that. You see the way things work out for me, don't you?"

She shook her head. "I see that one day you'll get married, and be a marvellous husband."

"I wish I could be your husband," he told her bluntly.

She sighed.

"Will you do something for me? Will you send for my carriage – Edward's carriage? I'm tired, and I don't want to be here any more. Once I am back in St James's Square the carriage can come back here, and Edward will know nothing until he is ready to leave."

"You can't go back alone," Hugh expostulated. "It's deucedly improper."

"Will you come with me, then? Afterwards you can return here with the carriage."

"But what do you think Edward's going to say, when he finds out you've left? He'll eat me alive."

"Please, Hugh."

"Oh, all right. But if it ends up with swords or pistols, you'll be the one to blame."

"It won't," she assured him, rather drearily. "It won't."

XXV.

It was one o'clock when Fanny got back to St James's Square. Warned that her mistress might turn up very late – or not until morning – Gabriele was surprised she had not been obliged to wait longer, and was eager to hear how things had gone, but Fanny told her that she was tired – that she had a headache, and wanted to be alone. She would get herself ready for bed, and see Gabriele in the morning.

Palpably disappointed the Belgian girl slipped away, and Fanny sat down. She started removing the pins from her hair, and brushing it. Perhaps she should simply take her clothes off and go to bed. She peered into the shadowy looking glass, touched by a cold awareness of what she had done. Not yet. She couldn't move yet.

Edward was not going to forgive her, ever, for leaving his sister's house, but she had had no choice. No choice at all. One of the candles started guttering, and she snuffed it out.

Her windows looked on to the garden at the back of the house, but one casement was open and shortly after two o'clock she heard the distant clatter of carriages moving through the streets, going home. Perhaps from Grosvenor Square.

Somewhere in the room a clock was ticking and once she heard the cry of a watchman, but there was no futher sound. Until about half past two, when her ears caught the rumble of another vehicle, this time approaching round the square. Wheels ground harshly on cobbles and she even heard the horses' feet slither a little, as if they had been pulled up rather sharply. A carriage door banged, and moments later there was the murmur of a porter's voice. Then silence.

Wearily, Fanny looked down at her golden gauze. When she was sure that Edward had gone to his room she would undress and lie down, even if she stood no chance of getting to sleep.

The door opened without any warning whatsoever. Her breath catching in her throat, she stood up and turned to find Edward standing in front of her. His face was faintly flushed, and his eyes glittered. For several seconds neither of them spoke, then he closed the door behind him.

"Well. . . my dear Lady Ordley. Pray tell me, did you plan to affront my sister? Or was the whole force of the insult meant for me?"

"Edward. . . ."

"One can only hope you are happy with the effect of your actions. Georgiana distressed – my brother Hugh made to look like a callow youth, helplessly obedient to the woman he believes himself to be in love with. And there you sit, before your mirror. I understood it was exhaustion that drove you home, but I had no belief in that, so it's hardly a surprise to find you not yet gone to bed. I imagine you are admiring your image in that glass. Reflecting on your triumphs, perhaps."

"I was tired," she said quietly. "I had danced a great deal. And - " She realised suddenly that she didn't feel nervous any more. "There seemed little likelihood that I would see you again, my lord, until such time as you chose to go home. Hugh was very kind and I was grateful for that, since I had been abandoned by my husband."

"Abandoned? By me? I spent much of the evening going in search of you, but it seemed you were determined to engage in every dance, and of course you found no shortage of eager partners. I heard you – my wife – talked about on every side. So beautiful. . . . No doubt you received more compliments, during the course of this evening, than most women receive in a lifetime."

She moved a little towards him, where he was leaning as if for support against the door frame. She knew they were embarked upon bitter hostilities, and it drove the colour out of her face.

"And you?" she asked quietly. "What about the lovely Lady Jane? So appealing in the moonlight, with all that golden hair, and those pretty little feet in silver slippers. I understand that she is devoted to you – when she thought you might have been left for dead on the battlefield she shed such copious tears that your sister hardly knew what to do with her."

"Really?" His face was a frozen mask.

"You must be aware that Georgiana has been making plans. Jane comes from an ancient and wealthy family, and you all know one another so well. If you had not been so unfortunate as to meet me, or rather to have me thrust upon you through the vulgarity of a relative – *my* relative - you might even now be announcing your betrothal with the assistance of the *Times*, the *Gazette* and the *Morning Post*."

There was a long silence.

"Lady Jane is no concern of yours," he said at last.

"Perhaps not, but it's very clear that she is your concern. In Dover Georgiana made it plain she thought our marriage likely to be illegal, and even plainer that she hoped it might be. At the time I supposed this was only because she thought me not good enough, but I now realise there was a more precise reason." She stopped, gathering strength. "Perhaps I should inform you – if you are not aware of it – that she had, in any case, no need to feel anxiety. Before agreeing to be married, I told Mr Beresford and Captain Sulimann that I was afraid you could not fully understand what was being done and might later come to regret it, whereupon I was advised that such a marriage could easily be annulled, just so long as it had not been consummated. And if – if you have sometimes been irked because I would not tumble easily into your bed, then that, my lord, is your answer."

He stared at her, out of the shadows, as if he had never seen her before.

"What?"

"You may soon be free to marry Jane Armitage, or anyone else that pleases you, and all of this can be at an end."

"Are you telling me that you – personally – desire our marriage to be declared null and void?"

"It was never a marriage, Edward. You had a high fever, and an idea in your head that I needed to be rescued - from Lady Mapelforth, from having to earn my living. You were not thinking very clearly and I don't believe you expected to survive. You said so, afterwards."

Still leaning against the door, he looked blankly into her face.

"I was being a little rash, wasn't I? I could have left quite a mess behind."

"Well. . . if you – if you had never come home to England, then Hugh would have inherited everything. I might have been accepted as the Dowager Marchioness and allowed to occupy a comfortable situation, but I would not have *interfered* with anything. And I would have been rescued from my previous style of life, which – which I think was important to you. At the time." She went on quickly. "But you did not anticipate this present situation, and it cannot be allowed to continue. You must, I think, apply to the Archbishop of Canterbury."

Edward Ordley looked down at the rug beneath his feet.

"The Archbishop of Canterbury."

"I believe so."

He abandoned the support of the door, and came closer to her.

"Madam, neither the Archbishop of Canterbury, nor the Pope of Rome nor any other prelate shall be permitted to involve himself in my personal affairs."

"You don't understand – "

"No. My mind is befogged, and where there is fog one must have clearance. Not been consummated, you said? Well, we can always do something about that, can't we?"

Before she could make any move to avoid him he had reached out and caught her by the shoulders, dragging her up against him. Her ribs seemed to be cracking and she felt excruciating pain as his fingers dug themselves into the soft flesh of her arms, but when she tried to push him away he seized her hands and flung them aside, pinioning the arms behind her back. With a single movement he tore the gauze from her shoulders and began covering her throat with hot, angry kisses.

"Were you sorry for me?" he demanded. "Was that it? Perhaps the advantages – those you mentioned just now – perhaps they did matter a little, only not if I were going to be part of the deal. 'Till death us do part. . . .' What did that mean to you, Fanny?"

"Please," she whispered. "You're hurting me."

"I'll hurt you more before I've finished, my lady."

He forced her face close to his, so that he could stare at the tears streaming from her eyes, then he savaged her lips. By the light of the guttering candles she could see his own eyes glittering with fury and resentment. The eyes of a stranger.

"If only I had behaved like a gentleman, and made you a widow that night! You could have gone back to England and forgotten about me. Or would you have played the bereaved wife, perhaps, and claimed what was due to you. . . ."

She tried to turn her head away, but was not allowed to do so.

"I wonder which rôle would have suited you best - my red headed, green eyed witch!"

They had been standing close to the bed and suddenly he flung her backwards, on to the counterpane, but as he started to remove his cravat and velvet coat she made one last desperate effort.

"Edward, you're drunk! You don't know what you're doing – "

"Don't I? Well, in that case I cannot be responsible for my actions. Perhaps I should try getting drunk more often."

Frozen into immobility, she watched as he blew the candles out. When just one was left, on the table beside the bed, he came and stood looking down at her. By the flickering yellow light he could see her stricken eyes and colourless face.

"Oh, go to bed," he said suddenly, harshly. "Go to sleep. And dream sweet dreams if you dare!"

XXVI

A little after seven o'clock Gabriele looked into her mistress's room. Daylight was streaming between the partly drawn curtains and she went to pull them further back. Then she glanced towards the bed, and uttered a small shriek.

Fanny was lying on the bed in a huddled position. She was still wearing her golden dress, which was very obviously torn, and when she looked round her eyes seemed blank and empty.

"Miladi, what is wrong?" Gabriele ran across to her. "Oh, but your beautiful dress. . . ." Seeing that her mistress was shivering, she fetched a warm velvet dressing-cape and put it about her shoulders. "I will bring your chocolate, madame – "

"No – no, please. Bring me tea. Very strong tea."

When Gabriele came back she noticed at once the livid bruise at the corner of Fanny's mouth. Shakily she said that she had a very excellent salve which would have an effect upon the bruise, but as she was leaving the room Fanny asked her to wait for a moment.

"Gabriele, you must say nothing of this to anyone, you understand?"

"No. . . no, madame, I swear."

"Please do not forget." Fanny took a sip of tea, then wearily she lay back against her pillows.

She didn't feel as if she would be able to sleep for a very long time, but once she had drunk more tea and Gabriele had done her best with the healing balm – a precious possession brought from Belgium - her eyelids began to droop. Very gently the maid placed a cover over her, then all the curtains were drawn and she was left alone.

When she woke it was afternoon, and she knew that she felt better. Gabriele brought her a light luncheon, and at the same time dropped a letter on to the table.

"It is from Monsieur le Marquis."

Fanny picked the letter up. She was reluctant to break her husband's heavy seal, but at the same time she needed to know what the letter contained. It was, she saw, fairly brief.

'My dear Fanny,
'Gabriele tells me you are resting, so I will not disturb you, but it is now time to be out of London and it has come into my mind that we should leave for Ordley the day after to-morrow. If your maid requires advice about necessary arrangements she should speak with Caxton.

To-morrow evening I am engaged to visit the Haymarket opera with a small party, and hope you will feel able to go with me. If you should prefer not to do this perhaps you will be good enough to let me know. If I hear nothing, I shall expect the honour of your company.

It was signed, quite simply: 'Edward.'

The letter was astonishing, Fanny thought. It contained no hint of anxiety or even apology, no suggestion the writer felt regret. Hastily she folded it, tucking it out of sight. She couldn't bear to look at it or think about it.

In the end, though, she couldn't frame a reply either, and as the hours passed knew that she would probably have to attend the Haymarket Theatre. Not only because she could not write to her husband, but because she didn't want to hide away. Eventually she penned a hurried note to Georgiana, regretting the sudden exhaustion that had obliged her to leave the Victory Ball, and within an hour or so had received the expected meaningless response.

'. . . *my dearest sister, don't trouble yourself for a moment. We women are feeble creatures, and I own I have sometimes been obliged to do the very same. . . . I trust that you are now perfectly recovered.*'

The following evening she dressed carefully in a gown of soft blue lustring. Gabriele did remarkable things with her hair and almost managed to obscure the revealing bruise beside her mouth, but she was noticeably pale and because she didn't want her misery placed on public view she made sure her lips and cheeks were lightly rouged, even though Gabriele did not think it altogether right.

At the appointed hour she emerged from her room and found Edward waiting for her, just as he had on the night of the ball. He looked up when she appeared, and she saw something like admiration in his face, but his expression swiftly became less readable. Firmly she looked back at him, and he bowed.

"I hope you are well."

"Yes – yes, I'm very well, Edward."

In the carriage she kept her head turned away from him, and the silence between them lasted until they were almost at the theatre, when suddenly she felt his eyes upon her.

"Will you allow me, at least, to say that I'm sorry?"

"You may say anything you please, my lord."

The carriage stopped, the door was opened and a servant hurried to put up steps. For an hour or two at least, she would not be alone with Edward.

She had imagined the party they were joining would consist mainly of unfamiliar faces, but when they entered the box she saw at once that Hugh was there, and Georgiana. It was a small group, and of the two others present one was a stony faced dowager, the Countess of Reith, the other a young girl who was said to be her ladyship's granddaughter.

As the girl was presented to her, Fanny had no trouble at all in recognising the beauty who had sat beside her husband in the garden at Grosvenor Square. At close quarters Jane Armitage was even more strikingly lovely than she had appeared at a distance, but she said almost nothing, though her troubled blue eyes watched Fanny's face with something that could have been bewilderment. Beyond a single dismissive nod, her grandmother gave no sign of having noticed that Lord Ordley was accompanied by his wife.

They took their places and Fanny fixed her mind on looking round the theatre, which was nearly full. Under normal circumstances there would not have been a performance so late in the summer, but this year many things were different and Beethoven's *Fidelio* was evidently being offered as some sort of balm for society's tangled emotions. Fanny stared up at the theatre's flame coloured ceiling, then at the crowded boxes. A good many pairs of eyes were turned in their direction, but that didn't trouble her. She felt too numb.

On her left hand, Edward gazed thoughtfully at the curtained stage. Hugh had been obliged to place himself between Lady Reith and her granddaughter, but before taking his seat he had leant towards Fanny, asking quietly if she was recovered.

"Edward said you were not well." His handsome face looked troubled, and she forced a bright smile.

"I was tired, but now I am quite myself again. I. . . ." Her voice dropped. "I was very foolish the other night, and must beg your pardon."

Hugh glanced at his brother's averted face. "No, Fanny, you were not foolish. And I was only too happy - "

But at that moment the curtains began drawing apart, and he left the rest unsaid. Noisy chatter faded, leaving a small trail of whispers and coughs, and the performance began.

Fanny had never witnessed an opera before. Lady Mapelforth hadn't favoured such entertainment and Giles Templeton's rare visits to London had not usually taken in anything much beyond St Paul's and the Parthenon marbles. Under ordinary circumstances she would have derived immense pleasure from the performance, but Beethoven's music soon began to touch feelings that might have been better left undisturbed, and she started to wish she had stayed in St James's Square.

Edward sat beside her, so close that they might have linked hands without anyone being aware of it, but once he had ensured that she was comfortable and had an adequate view of the stage he turned to Lady Reith, who was seated on his other side, and for at least an hour the Countess received all his available attention.

During an interval in the performance Fanny sipped from a glass of wine, but she refused all offers of food and Georgiana remarked audibly that her new sister was not at all in looks, and probably had a chill coming on.

When the curtain finally descended there was prolonged applause, followed by a rustle of movement as chairs were pulled back and wraps gathered up. Georgiana said brightly that she hoped everyone would be going back to Grosvenor Square for supper, but Lady Reith declared that she was fatigued and could not think of staying out any longer - and Jane, of course, would have to go back with her. She would look forward to seeing Georgiana again in a fortnight's time, when she believed they would both be guests at Chatsworth in Derbyshire.

Georgiana seemed rather well pleased by this. After all, supper might not have been a very good idea. Fanny did not seem to be feeling the thing, and they were all tired – she ought to confess that only the day before she had scarcely known how to stand upon her feet. When spring came they would do it all again, and spend a delightful evening together.

They walked back along a crowded gallery, and down the stairs. As Fanny climbed into her husband's carriage she felt his hand beneath her elbow, but when she looked she saw that he had gone to join the Countess and Lady Jane, and Hugh came across and stood beside the open door of the equipage.

"Fanny. . . ." He was frowning. "You are going to Ordley, are you not, within the next day or so? Edward mentioned it the other evening, but when I asked him just now he as good as refused to answer me."

"I don't know." She managed to smile. "But I am sure that everything will be sorted out soon."

His eyes were on her face, and she realised he had noticed the obstinate blemish that still marred one corner of her mouth. It was beginning to fade, but so far had resisted every attempt at concealment. Hugh's gaze swung round to his brother, and there was nothing particularly friendly about the sudden directness of his look. The Countess and her granddaughter had just been assisted into their own vehicle, and Edward Ordley was standing to watch the heavy barouche roll away.

With a bow, Hugh said he trusted it would not be long before he had the very great pleasure of seeing Fanny again. Then he took his leave and walked over to join his brother, who was now engaged in seeing Georgiana on her way.

One by one the carriages pulled in, took up their burdens and rolled away again. Through the smoky torchlight Fanny saw Hugh talking to his brother, probably about the business of going to Ordley, and once again she wished she had not come out at all. She wished she could have been many miles away, and knew that something in her life had to change very quickly.

Eventually Edward joined her, and they drove away. During the brief journey he spoke very little, and she could think of nothing to say. Though she might not have admitted it, even to herself, during the last two days she had been conscious of a feeling that everything might not be lost – that Edward might, in his own way, love her – but to-night all that had been decimated. She had seen him with Jane Armitage and her grandmother, she had watched as he ignored the Dowager's contempt for herself. There was nothing more for them to talk about.

Back in St James's Square his lordship said something to Batsford, then he disappeared into the library, while Fanny went to her own room. Having told Gabriele she would not be needed again that night, she flung herself on to the bed and broke into a torrent of weeping. When the tears stopped, she lay awake for a long time. But she knew there was no danger she would be disturbed.

In the morning, Fanny scribbled a hasty note.

'My lord. . . I hope we can now talk about the necessity of ending our regrettable marriage. You had rather have taken a different wife. And I should like very much to be free.'

Her pen wavered at this point and for a second she shut her eyes, but the signature was added. She folded the note, sealed it and handed it to Gabriele with the direction that it should be passed immediately to his lordship.

Minutes later, as Fanny was staring bleakly at her breakfast chocolate, Gabriele came back into the room.

"Madame. . . ."

Fanny turned her head. "Yes? What is it?"

"Monsieur le Marquis is not here. He went out very early, before the sun rose. He took nothing with him, and Monsieur Caxton does not know where he has gone."

XXVII

Lord Ordley, it emerged, had taken a horse from the stables, but as the hours passed it became increasingly clear that he had not gone for a morning ride.

Pacing up and down in her own room, Fanny soon decided that he had simply travelled to one to one of his other houses. If he had done that, he would not have required to take anything with him. But she was aware that the servants were shocked. Lord Ordley, after all, was now a married man and it was perfectly plain that her ladyship knew little more than they did.

She did know something, though - she knew that he regretted his recent marriage. In fact, she suspected that he regretted it bitterly. He might be planning to do as she had suggested and obtain an annulment, and in such a case would almost certainly begin by removing himself from St James's Square.

But as the morning went on she started to wonder if something different might lie behind her husband's sudden disappearance. Her blood ran cold as she thought about the sort of thing that could have occurred. Riding in the park so early he might have been attacked by footpads. His strength not fully restored, he could have been overwhelmed and left in the bushes, while his attackers ran off with whatever valuables he might have been carrying.

Several times Fanny wanted to say something, perhaps to Batsford, to suggest a search. But she didn't do so, because common sense told her it would be absurd. Wherever her husband might be, she had no real doubt that he was there for some perfectly sound reason of his own.

The mellow days of summer were slipping away, and for a short time that afternoon rain poured down, dancing noisily in the gutters and reminding Fanny of the hours before Waterloo. Late in the afternoon a letter was handed to her, and for one second she thought it might be from Edward, then she saw the scrawled direction. It was a message from Lady Mapelforth.

Her ladyship wrote to say that just lately she had become very bored with being in England again. Everyone – who had not gone abroad – was now about to be stuck in the country for months on end, and she was not at all sure she could endure it. Therefore, she had arrived at a decision. She had heard from an old friend in Italy – Fanny must have heard her speak about the Princess d'Estrelini. The Princess had invited her to stay in Venice for the whole of the winter, and she had to confess that she had accepted at once. Her only regret was that things were not as they had been, for the Princess insisted she mustn't hesitate to take some friend or companion with her, and now that her dearest Fanny had been wrenched away she could not for the life of her think of anyone. . . .

The letter rambled on, going into detail about the friends with whom she was staying in Oxfordshire, but an idea was taking shape inside Fanny's head.

Edward might or might not be planning to seek an annulment of their marriage, but there was no doubt that he felt he had taken on some kind of sacred obligation and even if the legal bond were to be broken would probably insist there should be some kind of settlement upon his rejected wife. If, however, she were to go – make herself independent without any further delay – that burden would be lifted from his life and from his conscience. It was time, more than time that she took matters into her own hands.

If her former employer would accept her, she would go to Venice with Lady Mapelforth. If not she would immediately seek some other sort of post, either as a governess or as companion to some lady in society. There would be those who would resolutely avoid any contact with the former Marchioness of Ordley, but there would be others – many others – who would be happy to give her employment.

She hesitated for several long hours. But when evening came and still there was no sign of Edward, she sat down at an escritoire and began her letter to Lady Mapelforth. It was not an easy thing to write and after covering just half a sheet of paper she tore it up and began again. In the end she said more than she had intended to say – revealed more than she had intended to reveal – but with Lady Mapelforth concealment was not really going to be possible. The whole process took more than half an hour, but at last she read the letter through, signed it and was just about to seal it down when a sudden commotion distracted her attention.

"Oh, for heaven's sake! Such stupidity is beyond belief! Now, where is Lady Ordley?"

Fanny would have known her sister-in-law's voice anywhere, so she had a few moments of warning before the door opened and Batsford announced the Duchess of Knaresborough. Standing in the doorway, Georgiana looked around as if searching for something.

"Well, now you must tell me! What is the truth of all this?"

"What do you mean. . . ?"

"I mean, is it true that my brother Edward disappeared before dawn this morning, carrying with him only a brace of pistols?"

"*Pistols?*"

"I imagine you must know what on earth he would be doing with duelling pistols?" The Duchess's voice was sharp, but there was a faint tremor behind it.

Most of the colour had drained from Fanny's face. She knew she must not allow herself to faint, but for a moment or two the room moved around her.

"I didn't know about the pistols."

Georgiana appeared to grit her teeth. "What *do* you know?"

"I last saw Edward last night. After we got back from the theatre. Then. . . this morning Caxton told my maid that he had left the house before sunrise and taken a horse from the stables. Caxton said he had no baggage – or anything – with him."

"And you asked no other questions? Good God, why do you think a gentleman leaves his London house at that hour of the morning, without a word to anybody? I have known Batsford since I was a child, and I knew the truth as soon as I looked at him." She sat down rather suddenly on a satin-covered couch. "I knew already, though. I heard him last night, talking to Hugh. The Duke said it would not be of any consequence, but I was never more worried. This morning I sent a note round to Hugh's lodging, but when the servant came back he said my brother was not at home. Knaresborough had gone to his Club and I was in utter panic, but I told myself I might be wrong. . . then I could bear it no longer, so I came over here. Batsford tried to cover the truth, but it was in his face. And when he told me about the pistols. . . . I had so hoped I was wrong, and now – "

"You really believe," Fanny said, "that Edward has gone to fight a duel with his brother?"

"Of course he has. What else? It's your fault. . . ." Her dark eyes flashed vengefully at Fanny. "First you seduced Edward into marrying you, then you batted your lashes at Hugh and caused him to think you ill used. I hope you are happy with the disaster you have caused."

Fanny was struggling to think, fighting against the darkness closing round her.

"If they did – fight one another, it would have been early this morning. Wouldn't it?"

"I imagine so. Who knows? Who knows whether – " She shuddered violently. "At this very moment – oh God, I can't think about it. They are both my brothers."

Fanny rang the bell, and when a maid appeared she asked that Batsford and Caxton should be sent in at once.

"And bring a glass of water for her Grace."

"I don't want any water," Georgiana snapped as the door behind her closed.

"You are upset," Fanny pointed out. "And we have to think clearly."

Batsford and Caxton appeared very swiftly, and the valet told his story. My lord had been up quite late, writing letters and attending to business, then he had given directions that he should be woken no later than four o'clock. When morning came he had called for riding clothes, and a horse had been saddled up.

"And he told you something?" Georgiana put in.

"No, your Grace."

"He must have done. Gentlemen talk to their valets."

Caxton was silent.

"But you saw him take the pistols."

There was another pause, and then Fanny said quietly: "I know you are loyal to his lordship and don't wish to betray his confidence, but you told Batsford something. And that must have been because you were worried."

Caxton hesitated. "Yes. . . well, my lady, I did see his lordship take a brace of pistols. But he told me naught about what they were for."

Georgiana clenched her small fists in a gesture of frustrated anguish.

"There must have been something, though," Fanny persisted. "Something he said. He may be in very grave danger. Please think."

"He were going out of London, my lady."

They all stared at him.

"Are you sure?" Fanny asked.

"By six o'clock, he reckoned he'd be out of town."

"Wimbledon Common," Georgiana murmured. And she dropped

her head into her hands.

Somewhere a door closed, and out in the hall a young footman could be heard addressing someone deferentially. Fanny remained very still, but Georgiana jumped to her feet. Then the drawing room door opened, and Lord Ordley stood regarding the group in front of him.

XXVIII

Fanny remained in her room until she was sure Georgiana had gone, by which time it was past ten o'clock.

She had stayed in the drawing room just long enough to be sure that Edward was unharmed, then while Georgiana - not for the first time - wept theatrically, had followed the example of Batsford and Caxton, and removed herself from sight. Only after the Duchess's barouche had been heard to move away did she decide to emerge from her room.

Informed that Lord Ordley was in his library, she went directly there and after a moment of hesitation walked inside. Her husband was seated by the big writing table and at first she thought he was studying something, then she saw he was merely deep in thought. He did not look round as she entered, but when she moved closer he got to his feet.

"I have been reading the letter you sent me," he told her abruptly.

She had almost forgotten the letter, but was glad – she told herself - that he had read it.

"I wrote it this morning."

"Well, I imagine it was before you made the happy discovery that I might have been despatched by my brother."

"I never really believed you and Hugh would fight one another."

"Did you not?" He shot her a curious look. "How little you must know about men. It was my brother, of course, who threw out the challenge – "

"You mean. . . there was a duel?"

"If you could call it that. I was aware that Hugh had no intention of killing me, but I had an idea he rather favoured the thought of being killed himself. I decided to humour him, but only so far. I undertook to provide the weapons - those pistols belonged to my late father. A very fine brace, made by Trevey."

"I cannot believe that Hugh – "

"Hugh was damnably low. Besotted with you, seeing nothing much in the future beyond duns and gaming tables, he no doubt thought the best thing he could do was take leave of this world. He would rather have liked to perish at Waterloo, but that chance being gone -"

"Don't!" Fanny felt sickened. "Why – why did he want to fight you?"

Edward Ordley's eyebrows rose. "To teach me a lesson. To punish me for monstrous behaviour, for my 'ungentlemanly' treatment of you. I think, to punish my temerity in marrying you. Actually, I'm not sure how it was going to work, for he was the one not supposed to survive. No doubt, though, my life thereafter was expected to be marred by guilt. As it would have been, I daresay, only I fired into the air. As he did."

"And then it was over?"

"You appear disappointed." His smile glimmered unpleasantly. "Well, I suppose many women would be."

"I just want to be sure that such a – such a nonsensical thing will never happen again."

"As my former tutor used to remark, 'never' is a word best handled with discretion. But no, I don't believe Hugh and I will get to such a stage again. We had a sensible discussion, and shook hands upon it. Now he is gone down into Kent, to stay with the family of a brother officer." He glanced at Fanny. "To-morrow you and I should have a candid talk, but for now. . . . Your looks suggest that you need, perhaps, more rest. You are thinner than you were, and also somewhat pale."

"My looks!" Normally she would have allowed such a

comment to pass unnoticed, but in the circumstances she felt as if she had been stung.

"As you are perfectly well aware, I was referring to the fragility of your appearance."

"I have been worried, Edward."

The words were out before she could stop them, but despite the quiver in her voice his dark eyes flashed her a look of undisguised hostility.

"Worried? Are you sure?"

"Of course."

"Well, forgive my stupidity, but I should have imagined my absence would be a source of relief. Even the news of my demise. It would, after all, have solved so many difficulties."

"How can you say that after - after - "

"After all your devotion? All those hours when you sat beside me, never complaining, always there? Well, yes, I can say it because we should never have been married, and your devotion should never have been called for."

Fanny jumped to her feet, in the process knocking over an untouched glass of wine, sending its contents cascading over the highly polished surface of her husband's desk.

"I asked for an annulment, my lord." Her voice was shaking. "I didn't ask for your insults, and I – I shall be glad if you will not trouble me again until we can speak in the presence of an lawyer."

She rushed to the door and tugged it open. Outside in the hall two discreetly unobservant footmen were on duty in the shade of the Corinthian columns, and before passing them she tried to compose herself, but it wasn't possible. She ran up the stairs and across the gallery to her own room, where she very firmly turned the key in the lock.

Gabriele – who had been suffering from toothache – had been sent to her own room hours before, and this was a relief because at that moment Fanny could not have spoken to anyone. It was several minutes before she felt calm enough to think about getting herself ready for bed, but eventually she let her hair down, undressed and climbed into the huge four poster that had once belonged to her husband's mother. Her satin night gown was trimmed heavily with lace, and she recalled the morning when she had bought it, and the thoughts that had drifted through her head. Then she snuffed all but one of the candles, and pressed her damp cheeks into a cool pillow.

She had been in bed no more than five minutes when she heard the door handle begin to turn. The movement was gentle at first, but it rapidly became more energetic. Then it was followed by a peremptory knock.

Beginning to shake, Fanny sat up in bed.

"Open this door, my lady, or I'll break it down," the Marquis ordered. When there was no immediate response his fists began pounding against the fragile woodwork, and Fanny jumped out of bed.

"I don't," his lordship told her, "wish to arouse the whole house, but if it becomes necessary I shall not hesitate to do so. Turn the key in the lock, Fanny."

Fanny didn't move or answer, and a sharp kick hit one of the lower panels. Probably this was intended as no more than a warning, but the door seemed to rock on its hinges.

Then there were other voices outside. Mrs Roper, and a housemaid. Batsford, saying that he might be able to find another key, but of course if her ladyship - one would hesitate. . . .

Able to endure no more, Fanny decided she would put an end to the whole ridiculous farce. With a burst of anger – which quite overcame the trembling in her limbs – she walked to the door and flung it wide.

Hastily Batsford stepped back. Mrs Roper, who was wearing a night cap and an old fashioned, voluminous robe, stood looking anxiously from Fanny to the Marquis, who was leaning against a wall with his arms folded.

"We thought there might be – perhaps there might be something wrong, my lady," Batsford explained apologetically.

Without so much as a tremor in her voice, Fanny assured

him that there was nothing in the least wrong.

"I must have been rather deeply asleep," she told them calmly. "And my door does stick a little. Perhaps, Mrs Roper, you will see that something is done about it."

"Very good, my lady." The housekeeper shot a somewhat dubious glance at her master. "And there is nothing wrong, my lady?"

"Nothing," Fanny assured her. "I'm so sorry you were disturbed," she added.

"Well. . . I wish you a good night, my lady."

Fanny inclined her head. "Good night, Mrs Roper. Good night, Batsford."

As they both appeared inclined to linger there was only one thing Fanny could do, and that was stand aside for his lordship to enter. When he had done so she closed the door and turned to confront him, and was astonished to see his eyes dancing with laughter.

"That," he observed, "should teach you a lesson. But I must say, you delivered a truly magnificent piece of acting. I don't believe I've seen anything come up to it, not at Drury Lane."

Fanny's lips started to tremble. Now that there was no longer any real need to maintain her dignity, large tears had begun rolling painfully down her cheeks.

"Come here, my foolish little love," Edward Ordley said huskily.

He held his arms out to her, and she hurled herself into them.

"Oh, Edward," she sobbed. "Oh, Edward. . . Edward!"

"I found your letter to Lady Mapelforth," he told her. "So you see, I understand. At last."

And for the next two or three minutes it was all he could do to check the storm of weeping.

XXIX

Hours later, Fanny stirred in her husband's arms. She was not sure whether he was awake or not, but she was content just to lie still and study the curve of his cheek. It had been daylight for a long time, but Gabriele had not yet made any attempt to enter. She had tapped on the door once, but there had been no response and after thinking carefully she had slipped away again.

Fanny became aware of the fact that Lord Ordley had opened his eyes and blinked.

"Are you awake, Edward?"

"I believe so." He turned his head on the pillow. "For a moment I thought I must be dreaming."

"I think it's quite late," she remarked with a contented sigh.

"Is it, indeed?"

"I don't believe I shall go to sleep again."

"Excellent," he drawled.

She could not repress a tiny laugh. "Yes, but I want to talk. You have not told me yet what really happened between you and your brother."

"Must I tell you?"

"Yes."

"Well, perhaps I must. If I don't do so Hugh will very likely tell you himself one of these days, though he had better be careful when he acquires a wife of his own. Whoever she turns out to be, I don't suppose it will take her long to realise that her husband's heart was once damaged by his beautiful sister-in-law."

"I don't believe Hugh's heart was damaged at all," Fanny said thoughtfully. "He may have fancied himself in love with me, but only because he is particularly susceptible. One day soon he will meet some charming girl, and everything will be forgotten."

"I bow to your better understanding of such matters," her husband observed, "but if Hugh was *not* in love, then he was putting on a good performance." He lifted himself on one elbow, and looked down at her. "The other evening, when we were all at the opera. . . that was when matters started getting out of hand. I suppose his feelings could be contained no longer."

"What happened?"

"After we left the theatre, he came over and asked if I did not think you seemed tired and unhappy. He also. . . I realised that he had noticed this." Suddenly sober, Edward bent and pressed his lips, very gently, to one corner of Fanny's mouth. "I was never more ashamed than when I saw the bruise myself, and I don't expect you to forgive me – "

"I have told you, Edward, I forgave you at once. It was not your fault. I know now that I had driven you nearly out of your mind by saying what I did."

"Well. . . I shall never quite forgive myself. As for Hugh, he called me a blackguard and called me out on the spot. There is no choice, in such a situation. I had to go through with the business."

"If I had been there - "

"It would have made no difference, sweetheart. Anyway, I had no intention of hitting him and I was perfectly certain he didn't intend to hit me. We arranged to meet near Sevenoaks, at a place known to us both. I was to bring a pair of weapons. That night we both managed to find seconds from among Army men who happened to be in town, and when morning came we all met in a damp field. Hugh and I fired into the air, and after that I persuaded him to talk. I told him the truth."

"Did you?"

"Yes. I said that I adored you, and had once believed you

might come to feel something for me. He said I should fight to keep you, which was noble of him, and so we went our separate ways."

Fanny lay in silence for a while, then she said: "Hugh will be leaving his regiment soon, or so he says."

"Yes. I shall place him in charge of a small estate and supply him with an income. After that, I shall expect him to manage his own affairs. He may very well marry an heiress, though. When we were growing up, as I well remember, our girl cousins invariably flocked around him."

"He says precisely the same about you, my lord."

"Does he, indeed?"

She stole a glance at his chin. "Jane Armitage, I'm sure, was always one of your admirers."

"Ah! I thought it would not be long before we came to the subject of Jane. You saw us together, didn't you? In Georgiana's garden."

"Yes."

"And you ran away. If you had not done that, you might have understood the situation better. Jane is – was – profoundly attached to a fellow called John Charteris, an officer in my own regiment. Charteris had little money and Lord Reith did not look on him with much favour, but. . . ."

"Yes?"

"It's all one now, I'm afraid. As you've probably guessed, he was killed at Waterloo. Quite naturally, I suppose, Jane wished to ask me questions about him. His last days, that sort of thing. Very few people knew that there had been an understanding between them – Hugh didn't, so when you and he saw us together he was not able to explain the situation to you."

Fanny was deeply shocked. She felt the keenest pity for Jane Armitage, who had lost so much while she had been so fortunate.

"I wish I had known," she murmured. "I feel ashamed."

"You have no need to be ashamed of anything, but I should have told you something about Jane, certainly before we all went to the opera together. I didn't honestly think you would suspect me of nourishing a *tendre* in that direction, although I realise now. . . ."

He ran a finger down the length of her nose. "I do understand that Georgiana has been trying quite hard to make you uncomfortable. I love her because she is my sister, but she can be very wilful and she wanted – I suppose – to choose my wife. Hugh warned me there would be trouble if I didn't do something about her. Anyway, I accused her last night. After you went upstairs."

"Accused her?"

"Yes. She shed a good many tears and confessed quite freely that she had wanted to change things. Only now that she knew you better, she realised how wrong she had been. She may be a schemer, but she knows when to stop. Richard Knaresborough has her nicely in hand, and he may have spoken a word. Anyway. . . ." He lay back against their pillows. "She can now fix her mind on finding a very rich wife for Hugh."

Fanny sighed. "I might not have been so stupid about everything, but you seemed so cold. At the opera you didn't talk to me at all. I thought – I was sure you regretted having married me."

"I had no doubt that you regretted marrying me. In fact, I was sure you wanted almost nothing to do with me. While I was still in a feeble state – that I could understand, but you seemed to draw away from me more and more. When I came home last night, I was not sure what to do. I had made up my mind to fight for you, but believed it was going to be a struggle. And then I saw your abandoned letter to Lady Mapelforth, and something told me I had to read it. I have never made a practice of reading other people's correspondence, but clearly there are moments when such things have to be done."

"Dear Lady Mapelforth," Fanny murmured. "She was very kind to me, and I shall always be grateful to her. One day, I should like her to come and stay with us. Would you mind, Edward?"

"You may invite whom you please, whenever you please." He looked at her broodingly, and pulled her closer. "But not for a little while yet."

XXX

Ten days later, at an hour when the September sun was just beginning to touch London's chimney pots, the Marquis of Ordley's travelling chariot slipped away from St James's Square. A second carriage and a baggage wagon followed behind, and the cavalcade was accompanied by several outriders.

Lady Ordley understood, vaguely, that they were heading towards Ordley in Hampshire, but her husband had been reticent about the details of their journey, declining absolutely to do more than assure her that they would reach Ordley eventually.

"Sweetheart, does it really matter?" Seated at his ease in a corner of the carriage, with his wife firmly locked in his arms, he could see no reason why, at such a moment, large amounts of information should be considered necessary. "All will be made clear in due course, and in the meantime I find this completely satisfying. Or very nearly satisfying. There are other things I might prefer to be doing if I had the choice."

She put back her head and looked up at him, noting among other things the way his dark eyes gleamed at her between their heavy lashes. She put a finger up and began tracing his lips with an appreciative finger tip.

"Edward," she murmured into his cravat, "I do love you so very much."

"I am extremely happy to hear that." He dropped a kiss on the top of her head – for reasons of his own he had requested her not to wear a bonnet while travelling inside the carriage.

211

"It's gratifying. And reassuring, especially as an annulment of our marriage might now be a little difficult to obtain, even if we should be fortunate enough to receive assistance from the Archbishop of Canterbury."

Fanny felt herself blushing, but her face was hidden and he was not in a position to notice. For some time neither of them spoke, then as the carriage rocked around a sharp bend he suddenly returned to the subject.

"Sweetheart, I know Georgiana questioned the validity of our marriage. She distressed you, and I could almost throttle her for that."

"She was upset also. She believed that you had made a mistake, and might be regretting it. She was – I suppose she was trying to think what could be done."

"Well, I have gone into the matter very thoroughly, and have been assured the ceremony was absolutely secure. During time of war, our chaplains are allowed to conduct such marriages. They need neither banns nor licenses. Old Beresford would have known that – would have done such things before, perhaps many times. It was what is sometimes known as a drumhead wedding."

"I like the sound of that."

"If we had been married in France the situation might have been different. Under Napoleon's *Code Civil*, marriage by a priest alone cannot be binding. But as ours was a ceremony conducted within the British military, it's unlikely there would have been a difficulty, even then."

The sun, by this time, was high in the sky. London, with its outlying villages and farms, woods and heathland had long been left behind and open countryside lay all round them. In the pale September light everything looked curiously untouched – or would have done, if it had not been for the very straight white road cleaving its way ahead.

"You did say that we were travelling towards Ordley, didn't you, Edward?" Crinkling her brows a little, Fanny peered out of the window.

"Yes, my love. We shall arrive there eventually."

"But this is the road to Dover. Unless I am very much mistaken, and I have travelled it on two occasions recently."

"No, my clever little wife, you are not mistaken." Indolently the Marquis tipped his curly brimmed beaver hat so that it shielded his eyes from the sun. "This is most certainly the Dover road."

"But Ordley is in quite a different direction."

"True," he agreed. "One cannot easily get to Hampshire by travelling through Dover. But Dover does lead to other things. Italy, for instance. . . . Switzerland, Vienna. Paris, even. Though before going there one would wish to be sure they had cleaned it up a bit. Have you ever been to Geneva?"

"No, but – "

"Athens?"

"Of course not."

"You do seem to have been deprived, my love, though if you had stayed with Lady Mapelforth I have no doubt you'd have seen it all eventually. As it is, you'll just have to put up with my company."

"You mean. . . ." Her eyes widened in disbelief. "We are returning to the continent?"

"For a little while. Two or three months, perhaps, according to my lady's pleasure."

"But Edward. . . ." She caught at his arm. "Why not Ordley? You have been wanting so much to see it again. And just now you said – "

"I said that we should reach Ordley eventually, and so we shall. When you are stronger, sweetheart, we'll go there and you will meet all my relations, and the neighbours among whom I grew up. On this occasion we won't travel too far, and we shall reach Ordley, I daresay, in time for Christmas. But until then you need to be protected – cherished - as you have never been in your life." He kissed the fingers he had been holding against his cheek. "Fanny, have I told you yet that I love you more than anything else in life?"

"Yes, my lord. I believe you have."

"And astonishingly, I think that just a short while ago you said that you loved me?"

"Yes, Edward."

"Then that, surely, is a matter for celebration. Within an hour or so we shall stop at the Bell in Canterbury, where we shall take some refreshment before travelling on to Dover. And to-morrow. . . to-morrow, Fanny, we shall be married again. By an English parish priest, in an English church overlooking the English Channel. Hugh will be there to act as one of our witnesses, and there will be Caxton. And, of course, your maid Gabriele. Your new ring will be properly blessed, and when we come back to England we will write that note to Cornet Faraday."

"But I thought – you said. . . ."

"I said we were already married, and that remains beyond doubt. But when you are blessed with my kind of relatives – and, unfortunately, my worldly possessions – every knot needs to be tied so securely no-one can pretend not to see it." He looked a little anxious. "You are not unhappy about the arrangement?"

"Of course not. . . of course not. Oh, Edward, you are utterly wonderful!"

Before they arrived at Dover, Lord Ordley recalled one more thing he had been meaning to tell his bride.

"By the way," he said, glancing at her face, "I have decided that Whitcombe Park should be made over to Freddie and Justine. Neither of them deserves such a gift – well, Freddie, perhaps – but my conscience won't permit me to do otherwise. Perhaps I should call it my sense of obligation. And I have a feeling you are going to be pleased."

This time, Fanny was bereft of words.

"I don't know how to thank you," she admitted at last.

"Then don't try," he advised. "Just leave it to me. I'm quite certain I shall think of a way."